GW 2540294 3

VERITY

By the same author

Elizabeth the Beloved
Kathryn, the Wanton Queen
Mary, the Infamous Queen
Bride for King James
Joan of the Lilies
Flower of the Greys
The Rose of Hever
Princess of Desire
Struggle for a Crown
Shadow of a Tudor
Seven for St Crispin's Day
The Cloistered Flame
The Woodville Wench
The Peacock Queen
Henry VIII and His Six Wives
Jewel of the Greys
The Maid of Judah
The Gallows Herd
Flawed Enchantress
So Fair and Foul a Queen
The Willow Maid
Curse of the Greys
The Queenmaker
Tansy
Kate Alanna
A Child Called Freedom
The Crystal and the Cloud
The Snow Blossom
Beggar Maid, Queen
I, The Maid
Night of the Willow
Ravenscar
Song for a Strolling Player
Frost on the Rose
Red Queen, White Queen
Imperial Harlot
My Lady Troubador
Lackland's Bride
My Philippa
Isabella, the She-Wolf
Fair Maid of Kent
The Vinegar Seed
The Vinegar Blossom
The Vinegar Tree
Lady for a Chevalier
My Catalina
The Noonday Queen
Incredible Fierce Desire
Wife in Waiting
Patchwork
Minstrel for a Valois
Witch Queen
Much Suspected of Me
Proud Bess
The Flower of Martinique
England's Mistress
A Masque of Brontës
Green Apple Burning
Child of Earth
Valentine
Child of Fire

VERITY

MAUREEN PETERS

ROBERT HALE · LONDON

First published in Great Britain 2002

ISBN 0 7090 7136 1

Robert Hale Limited
Clerkenwell House
Clerkenwell Green
London EC1R 0HT

2 4 6 8 10 9 7 5 3 1

Typeset in 11/13pt Baskerville
by Derek Doyle & Associates, Liverpool.
Printed in Great Britain by
St Edmundsbury Press Ltd, Bury St Edmunds, Suffolk.
Bound by Woolnough Bookbinding Limited.

ONE

The sitting-room of Tansy Clark's Chelsea home stretched from the front to the back of the building. A large bay window at the front gave a clear view of the small garden beyond which the quiet road curved past similar houses towards the cab-stand at the corner where it joined the main road. A pair of french windows at the back opened on to a narrow terrace from where steps descended to a long flower-bordered lawn that ran to a low stone wall separating the property from the river flowing past.

In quiet evenings when twilight lingered in the rose and mauve of the sleepy sky and the night-scented stock sent its perfume drifting on the breeze Tansy liked to open the windows and stroll in the garden. High walls thick with ivy hid the houses at each side and gave her the illusion that she was deep in the country.

This evening, however, she felt unaccountably restless. It had been a tranquil week. She had dined twice with her father, given out the prizes at the local church fête, read two library books and turned out her desk. She was, she told herself, a fortunate woman.

Right now she might be one of the many eking out a living as a factory-hand or shop-assistant or toiling away as governess in someone else's house. Instead of that she was possessed of a pleasant little house and an income sufficient for her modest needs – both willed to her by a fiancé who had died of yellow fever ten years previously before embarking on his voyage home from Jamaica in order to marry her. She was still the right side of thirty-five and, according to her housekeeper, Mrs Timothy, a handsome woman.

Handsome, Tansy thought now with an inward grimace, wasn't stylish these days. Smallness and daintiness were the most highly prized attributes of a woman and she was neither. A slender frame and white skin, excellent teeth and abounding good health didn't mitigate green eyes, strongly marked features or a mane of red hair. Neither did they alter her height or her wide mouth. Men liked young women who could nestle coyly in their arms. Tansy had never nestled in anyone's arms, not even in Geoffrey's. She had loved him but theirs had been a meeting of minds, a mutual craving for adventure. Yet ten years later she was still living in the home they had planned to share in between trips to the Far East and the Americas to collect material for Geoffrey's books.

None of that had happened. Tansy drank the rest of her wine, put the glass down on the pedestal of a stone vase near the steps and continued her stroll down the garden to the riverbank. She had more than a house and an income, she reminded herself. She had a father who paid her the compliment of treating her as an equal, a devoted and efficient housekeeper in the person of Mrs Timothy and a helpful maid-of-all-work who was called Tilde and luxuriated in the belief that she had French blood. And she had Frank – or did she?

Seating herself on the low wall she brought Frank's image into her mind. Thick fair hair, keen grey eyes, an unfashionably clean-shaven and tanned countenance, taller than herself with broad shoulders and long legs – still the right side of forty. And so far unattached, she reminded herself.

Not that that mattered one way or the other! She frowned as she mentally rubbed out his image, replacing it with her remembered one of Geoffrey, but the substitution wasn't entirely successful. Geoffrey had been sandy-haired, his features classical, his sideburns longer, but the face in her mind was growing dimmer as the years passed. She could recall the way he had walked or the sound of his voice only with some difficulty as if he were retreating into the shadows, moving further away from her present reality.

The truth was, she thought, that youthful loving was turning into mature regret for what might have been.

Suddenly impatient with the direction in which her thoughts were tending she swung herself round until she was gazing at the river and her glance dropped the three feet to the bank on the other side. A narrow track meandered past the adjoining gardens with the river flowing on the other side. Somewhere from the reeds that grew at the very edge of the water a kingfisher rose up and was gone in a flash of blue. Further along some otters had built a natural barrier of mud and silt dried by the summer sun, reinforced by sticks and trailing stems of water plants. She had seen the young otters playing on the riverbank with an anxious parent keeping a watchful eye on them. She had read somewhere that otters mated for life and wondered if that was true.

This evening the otters were nowhere to be seen. Tansy walked on, enjoying the light breeze that ruffled her hair. The thought that it would've been even more pleasant strolling here with someone at her side she brushed away. Frank was out of town, following up some story he would write for his newspaper. If he wasn't doing that then he was almost certainly with one of the pretty young women to whom he regularly lost his heart for varying periods of time.

Tansy rounded a bend and paused. Here the path became wider with the river curving away and itself widening, the splashing of its water over a water wheel making fresh music on the air.

A young woman was seated on the bench ahead of her, watching the water wheel as it turned slowly, scattering droplets. She had heard Tansy's approach, raising her head and turning slightly to look at her, one hand shading her eyes against the last flare of sunlight.

'Good evening,' she said.

Tansy, deciding it would look rude to turn back abruptly, bowed her head slightly with a smile and would have gone by but the other suddenly rose and took a couple of steps toward her.

'You are Miss Clark, are you not?' she said.

'I am but I don't believe I've had the pleasure of—' Tansy began.

'Mrs Simpson. Verity Simpson. We moved to Chelsea only recently and are not yet acquainted with our neighbours. It is quite hard to make new acquaintances in the city, don't you think? But your housekeeper – Mrs Timothy? – she was kind enough to give me directions to the church the other day. She mentioned that she worked for you and then the other morning I saw you walking down the road. I was too shy to make myself known to you but you were exactly as Mrs Timothy described.'

'Good heavens,' Tansy said, amused. 'I wonder what she said.'

'That you were tall and elegant with auburn hair,' the other told her.

'Mrs Timothy is apt to gild the lily,' Tansy said drily. 'I'm pleased to meet you, Mrs Simpson. I hope you're settling in?'

'Oh yes – yes, really quite well,' the other said. 'As John – John is my husband – says – Chelsea is hardly the city proper, is it? He tells me we must bide our time and not trouble strangers with overtures of friendship. I really ought not to be talking to you now, and interrupting your walk.'

'Someone has to offer the greeting first,' Tansy said. 'If you attend our local church and use the local tradespeople you will soon find yourself meeting people.'

'That's what John says,' Verity Simpson said.

There was a forlornness about her as she sat on the bench. Tansy, moved to sympathy, said,

'Meanwhile sitting by the river all alone cannot be the most cheerful of occupations.'

'No. No, I suppose not.' The young woman gave a little laugh that sounded curiously like a sob, 'My husband says the river depresses him greatly, but he is not naturally of a cheerful nature.'

'What is his occupation?' Tansy enquired.

'He is a writer.' There was a lilt of pride in the soft voice and the beginnings of a smile at the back of the blue eyes. 'Of course he is not yet established but that takes a long time, he tells me. It can be years before a writer becomes a household name. However he does become despondent sometimes so I feel it my duty to try to cheer him up. You did not meet him as you walked along?'

'Just now? No, I passed nobody.'

'I was hoping he might come.'

She gave a little sigh and bit her lip.

'Does he make a habit of walking along the riverbank?' Tansy asked.

'Occasionally he walks back this way when he has been into the city. He says that it is almost like taking a country stroll. He went into town this morning to see a publisher. He was rather hopeful that his work had been approved – perhaps the publisher invited him to stay for dinner, don't you think, Miss Clark?'

'I have no experience of the publishing world,' Tansy said, not pointing out that in her limited experience, gleaned mainly from Frank, publishers weren't in the habit of inviting unknown authors to stay for dinner.

'And I'm keeping you from your walk,' the other said in a hurried, apologetic tone that seemed to strive for cheerfulness and failed. 'I must go in and light the lamps. We have no servant yet so I am obliged to do most things myself. Good evening, Miss Clark.'

'Mrs Simpson.' Tansy bowed and watched the slight young figure walk through a nearby gateway and up through the tangled garden of a house that was somewhat larger than its neighbours.

Twenty-four or five, pretty in a fashionable way with large blue eyes and fair hair curled into ringlets. Nicely spoken, a mite timid.

At least, thought Tansy, as she retraced her steps back to her own garden, an unmarried woman wasn't obliged to sit about waiting for an absent husband to come home. There was some consolation in that for her single state!

When she reached her own sitting-room, sitting on the garden step to take off her shoes, Mrs Timothy bustled in after a brisk tap on the door.

'Getting chilly,' she observed.

'Nonsense! it's really quite warm,' Tansy said, coming in. 'I met a new neighbour by the by – Verity Simpson?'

'I met her a couple of days ago. She was over looking for the church,' her housekeeper said. 'Here are your slippers, Miss Tansy. She looked a bit lost so I stopped and asked if I could help. Nice young lady, I thought, but a bit bewildered-like. Reminded me of Tilde in a way.'

'Yes, possibly.' Tansy spoke slowly, considering the matter. Tilde was what Tansy's father liked to call 'one of your lame dogs' – a young girl whom she had come across seated on a park bench, having lost her situation, and rather melodramatically contemplating suicide in a few feet of water.

'You don't think so?'

'Tilde missed her calling when she didn't go on the stage,' Tansy said with a grin. 'She has lots of personality and nothing really keeps her down for long. I thought that Verity Simpson appeared quite melancholic by nature, and with far less to say.'

'Since half of what Tilde says is nonsense that might not be a drawback,' Mrs Timothy said darkly. 'Anything you want, miss?'

'I shall read a while and then have an early night,' Tansy said. 'You and Tilde go to bed whenever you choose.'

A pleasant small room behind the kitchen was Tilde's domain. Mrs Timothy occupied the larger room beyond with a small bathroom that Tansy had added between the rooms.

'You'll not forget to lock up?' Mrs Timothy said with a glance at the open french windows.

'No, of course not. 'Night, Mrs Timothy.'

' 'Night, Miss Tansy.'

The housekeeper heaved her solid frame out of the sitting-room. As Tansy locked the windows and drew the long curtains, she found herself wondering if the absent John Simpson had returned with good news for his young wife. It was, of course, none of her business but it was better than guessing which one of his regular conquests was enjoying Frank's attentions at the moment.

Her mind, she thought irritably, strayed far too often in Frank Cartwright's direction these days.

In the morning as she drank her coffee and discussed the day's menus with her housekeeper her attention still threatened to stray.

'Veal if you can manage to obtain some, Mrs Timothy, and some of those juicy red plums that Tilde was – which reminds me, since when was my hair auburn and my person elegant?'

'As long as I've 'ad the privilege of knowing you, Miss Tansy,' Mrs Timothy said without batting an eyelash.

'Well, try not to sing my praises all over Chelsea,' Tansy advised drily, 'or you will encourage the world and his wife to come knocking at the door in the hope that you speak the truth!'

'It was the truth, miss. I've often thought that shade of hair might suit me – give me a bit of a lift, but since I don't approve of dyeing—'

'Leave the henna bottle where it is,' Tansy said. 'Tell me, what do you know of our new neighbours? Not very near neighbours I admit as their house is some distance off.'

'Ten houses off,' Mrs Timothy nodded. 'The Larches – rather a nice tree when it's in full leaf but looks a mite untidy come autumn.'

'The house has been empty for some time, hasn't it?'

'Over a year, miss. Mr and Mrs Dewsbury went abroad. He had

a weak heart though I doubt if racketing about on the Rivie – what you call it—'

'Riviera,' Tansy supplied.

'That's the place. I cannot see how racketing about there can improve his heart. Bars and gambling!'

'The Prince of Wales frequently holidays there and the Queen also visits.'

'Does she indeed?' Mrs Timothy looked astonished. 'I'd've thought that since Prince Albert passed over – God bless him! – she'd not have fancied taking holidays.'

'The Larches . . .?' Tansy brought her back to the subject.

'It's only rented,' Mrs Timothy told her. 'Mrs Simpson told me that her husband's a writer and desirous of making his name in the world and yet he gets very downhearted sometimes.'

'She told me that too,' Tansy said. 'She seemed rather a sad young woman.'

'Lonely.' Mrs Timothy nodded.

'I might take a stroll along the riverbank in a little while,' Tansy said thoughtfully.

'Now don't you go feeling so sorry for her that she turns up for coffee three times a week!' Mrs Timothy warned.

'Pots,' said Tansy with a chuckle, 'have no business to be calling kettles black!'

The rest of the day yawned ahead of her anyway. She had made out the menus, discussed the shopping-list in detail, made a note to have a pair of walking-shoes repaired, and it was still short of ten.

In the end she slipped on a jacket, put on a straw hat and went out through the garden on to the river bank. She was most likely being very foolish, she scolded herself, since John Simpson was probably still regaling his wife with an account of a profitable interview with the publisher, but worrying about other people seemed to be another habit she'd picked up.

On the other hand, she told herself firmly, she was becoming far too accustomed to riding about in cabs, so a brisk walk would do her some good!

It was a beautiful morning with sunlight glinting off the surface of the river and dragonflies hovering amid the reeds. At this point the tumult of the great river had become a broad, sparkling stream.

When she reached the slowly turning water wheel she wasn't too surprised to hear a voice calling her or to see Verity Simpson, an apron tied around her narrow waist, tripping through the open gateway of The Larches.

'Good morning, Miss Clark! I am so glad you came by,' she said breathlessly, shifting a duster from one hand to the other as she came out upon the track.

'Good morning.' Tansy paused, struck by the expression on the pale pretty face. 'Something's wrong?'

'I'm in something of a quandary, Miss Clark,' the other said. 'John – my husband hasn't returned home since yesterday and I really don't know what to do!'

'He stayed away all night?'

'Yes, there's been no sight of him. I cannot think what to do!'

'Well, I'm hardly an expert on the subject of husbands . . .' Tansy began.

'You don't think the publishing gentleman may have invited him to stay overnight?'

'I think it highly unlikely,' Tansy said firmly. 'Of course he might have been wined and dined rather too well last night and, not wishing to distress you, decided to sleep over at an – hotel? He will very likely turn up later with a shocking headache.'

'John believes in moderation where the consumption of alcohol is concerned,' the girl said doubtfully. 'You don't think he may have had an accident?'

'Had he anything on him to denote his identity?'

'Oh yes, yes, I am sure he had!'

'Then someone would have notified you by now. No news is good news.'

'Oh, I do hope you're right!'

'He's not in the habit of staying out overnight?'

'Never! We've only been married a year!' Verity Simpson said earnestly.

Tansy mentally rubbed out the notion that John Simpson had strayed into some other bed and looked sympathetic.

'Perhaps he has good news and lingered to buy you a present,' she suggested and thought how unconvincing she sounded.

'The shops close overnight,' Verity Simpson said uncertainly, twisting the duster in her fingers. 'Miss Clark, you wouldn't like to come in for half an hour, would you? For a cup of coffee? I would be very grateful for a little company.'

'That's very kind of you,' Tansy said, mentally swallowing the excuse that had risen to her lips.

They walked together through the gateway which was, Tansy noticed, holding back a comment, quite useless with the posts sagging and the gate itself hanging uselessly. They went along a weedy path between high grass choked with brambles. The Simpsons were obviously not keen gardeners.

'The house isn't very tidy,' Verity Simpson said apologetically as she ushered her visitor through the back door. 'Please come.'

They went into a small dining-room with chairs and a table on which a coffee-pot was set.

'This is very convenient for the kitchen,' Tansy said politely, gingerly taking the chair the other had hastily brushed down with the corner of her apron.

'Yes. Yes, we find it so. Do you take sugar, Miss Clark? I forgot to buy milk. The truth is that I am still somewhat inexperienced in the management of a household. We shall get everything shipshape. We intend to have the place repainted! It is rather gloomy in here, don't you feel?'

'Noticeably so,' Tansy said, abandoning politeness for some measure of frankness as she looked round at the peeling wallpaper. Hastily she added, 'Of course you will soon have it to your liking! Have you no relatives near who could visit you?'

'None. My parents are both dead and so are John's. Oh, I do wish he would come!' Verity Simpson said tremulously.

'Did he mention which publisher he was going to see?' Tansy asked sipping the weak, milkless coffee.

'A Mr Oakley, I believe. Do you know him?'

'Not personally, no, but a friend of mine is an acquaintance of his. He might be able . . .' Tansy hesitated.

'Oh, if your friend could!'

'I take it your husband has already submitted a manuscript to him?' Tansy said.

'He did and that was why Mr Oakley wished to meet him.'

'Do you have a copy?'

Verity Simpson shook her head.

'John keeps his work very private,' she said. 'I don't even know the subject matter of his book.'

'Well, the most sensible thing to do would be to go to Mr

Oakley's offices and find out if your husband actually arrived there.' Tansy said briskly.

'Oh, I couldn't possibly!' The other looked horrified at the suggestion. 'No, I shall wait patiently and very soon John will come home with splendid news for me!'

'In that case,' Tansy rose, holding out her hand. 'I'll leave you to get on. As you say, your husband may well have some good news for you. Thank you for the coffee.'

'Let me show you out the front way!' Her hostess went ahead of her down a short corridor into a square hall where some effort had clearly been made to lighten the gloom. There were some rather wilted flowers on the hall table in a glass vase and the panels of stained glass in the top half of the front door had been polished to a shine. 'This is John!' Verity had darted into a front room, emerging with a photograph in a gilt frame.

'On your wedding day?' Tansy looked down at the two figures in the photograph as the other passed it to her.

The man standing beside the stool on which a veiled and flower-decked Verity sat was good-looking, his hair and moustache fair, one hand resting lightly on his bride's shoulder.

'We exchanged wedding rings,' Verity Simpson said softly. 'Mine has his name engraved within the band and his has my name which links us for ever.'

Had she ever been so young and so much in love, Tansy wondered? She had loved Geoffrey, been happy in his company, looked forward to being a wife, but sentiment had played a lesser role.

'John is utterly devoted to me,' Verity Simpson said.

Not if he stayed out all night without telling his bride where he was, Tansy thought cynically. Aloud she said,

'I'm sure you'll see him again very soon. Good day, Mrs Simpson.'

When she glanced back she saw her hostess still stood in the doorway, her fair head bent over the photograph.

TWO

'She looked so lost that I really felt sorry for her,' she confessed later in the day.

She was seated in the large comfortable first-floor sitting-cum-dining-room where her father spent most of his time. This was the house where she had been born and grown up, spending pleasant evenings by the fire while her mother, a piece of sewing in her hands, eagerly talked about her father's latest case. Laurence Clark had been a respected police officer whose work had earned him a reputation for skill and daring. She had grown up listening to her parents amicably wrangling about the possible solutions to various cases. After her mother's death she had become the one to whom he outlined his methods until a bullet had left him in a wheelchair from which he still took a keen interest in both past and current crime.

'Of course you must marry Geoffrey,' he had insisted. 'I shall look forward to spoiling the grandchildren.'

He and Geoffrey had got on well together, though Geoffrey's work had lain more in the field of archaeological research.

Then had come the news of Geoffrey's death and of his legacy to her.

'If you are thinking of selling the house then put the idea right out of your head,' Laurence had ordered her when the first grief was over. 'You're a young attractive woman and these days to lead an independent life is a course many young women are beginning to adopt. Call round and see me as often as you please but no nursemaiding!'

She had taken the advice, knowing that she was fortunate to have a pretty house and a modest income, knowing too that her father was well looked after by his manservant, Finn, who was pouring more coffee, a listening look on his long face.

'It sounds to me as if you've taken another lame duck under your wing,' her father teased now.

'No, indeed I haven't, Pa!' Tansy said energetically. 'Verity Simpson isn't interesting enough to be a lame duck of any kind. She is actually rather a silly kind of young woman if you ask me – the helpless sort.'

'Sounds to me,' said Finn, his long face lugubrious, 'as if John Simpson 'as done a bunk!'

'I hope not.' Tansy frowned slightly. 'She obviously adores him. I was wondering whether to advise her to go to the police.'

'What are you mixed up in now?' Frank's voice broke in as he appeared at the door.

'Hello Frank. I told Finn to leave the door ajar,' Laurence greeted him.

'I've closed it now since Tansy's already here,' Frank said. 'Good to see you again, sir! I'd been neglecting my friends of late but I decided to burn the midnight oil and get this latest batch of articles under way. How are you, Tansy?'

His lips brushed her cheek. To her own surprise Tansy felt her spirits rise. She said coolly,

'No need to apologize for neglecting your friends, Frank dear. The Lord knows you see little enough of them at the best of times.'

'What's ruffled your feathers?' He lifted an eyebrow at her.

'Tansy is worried about one of her neighbours.' Laurence speedily outlined the situation.

'It sounds as if he's deserted her,' was Frank's comment.

'But why?' Tansy demanded. 'She's a perfectly nice young woman, very pretty if a bit dull.'

'You said he's a writer. What kind of work does he do?'

'She didn't seem to know,' Tansy said. 'He keeps it private from her. He went to have dinner with Mr Oakley and never came home.'

'Oakley?' Frank accepted a drink from Finn and perched on the arm of Tansy's chair. 'He publishes quite weighty tomes on politics and theology and social philosophy. It's a small publishing house but well respected.'

'You know him, don't you?' Tansy said.

'Well enough to have the occasional game of billiards with him. Henry Oakley took over the firm from his late father and continued the same policy of publishing mainly non-fiction works of an erudite nature. I could ask him if he's recently seen a John Simpson if you like?'

'Would he be likely to ask an author to lunch or dinner?'

'He might if he believed he'd found an important new talent,' Frank said. 'Of course he may have written under another name. She didn't offer to show you the manuscript I suppose?'

'She didn't seem to know anything about the book or even if there was a copy of it,' Tansy told him.

'You think she should go to the police? A bit soon for that, isn't it?'

'Rather soon,' Laurence said consideringly. 'He's of full age and has the right to go where he chooses, wife or no wife. Unless he's breaking the law, of course. If he still hasn't returned during the next few days she could certainly make enquiries of them, but there isn't much they can do beyond checking the local hospitals, etcetera.'

'Oakley often dines at Wheeling's during the week,' Frank said. 'Tansy, do you fancy a meal out or is Mrs Timothy preparing a repast for you?'

'I told her that I was dining at Pa's,' Tansy said.

'In that case may I steal her away, sir?' Frank looked at the older man.

'By all means,' Laurence said genially. 'I'm becoming quite eager to discover the whereabouts of the errant John Simpson myself! No, you go along, girl! It will be more amusing for you to dine out than sit here with me and hash over stale gossip.'

'I'm not dressed for dining out,' Tansy began, glancing down at her lilac skirt and black-trimmed jacket.

'You look fine to me,' Frank said. 'Put your hat on and I'll call a cab.'

'And see that whatever you glean from Mr Oakley is reported back to me,' Laurence ordered. 'I need a new problem to solve.'

'We miss our crimes,' Finn said mournfully.

'He means the solving and not the committing of them,' Laurence said.

'In the latter I never 'ad much luck,' Finn agreed.

Outside Frank walked with her to the cab-stand, topping her

by several inches which was unusual for her when she walked even with a male companion.

'Did Pa tell you that I was going to be with him this evening?' she asked abruptly as he handed her into the vehicle.

'Why else would I have rushed there?'

'I do wish Pa would stop trying to arrange my social life! You might've had another engagement!'

'Which I'd've broken for the pleasure of seeing you!'

'You don't have to wait for Pa to invite you round in order see me,' Tansy said vigorously. 'You know perfectly well where I live!'

'I've been out of town. Anyway, why are you so interested in Mrs Simpson and her absent husband?'

He'd been with his latest conquest, she surmised. Not that it signified! Men were expected to sow their wild oats and women were supposed not to mind. She said brightly,

'I felt rather sorry for her!'

'You're a nice woman, Tansy Clark!'

'Nice,' Tansy thought with an inward grimace, was the highest compliment she could expect to receive from now on.

It was still almost light, the mellow glow of the gaslights competing with the streaked gold-shot evening sky. Within the cab the noises of the city were muted.

'Here we are!' Frank stepped out, paid the coachman and turned to assist Tansy, looking slightly nonplussed as he saw she had already alighted.

Entering the impeccable, restrained interior of Wheeling's she lectured herself on the desirability of staying inside the vehicle until either the coachman or her escort should have come to help her over the high step. The problem was that she was perfectly capable of climbing a five-barred gate and jumping down on the other side with no damage save to her stockings.

'What will you have?' Frank enquired when they were seated.

'*Saumon en croute* with vegetables,' Tansy said.

It looked expensive which would be a neat punishment for the unwanted compliment.

'And a bottle of very good wine,' Frank said placidly.

'Champagne?' Tansy inserted neatly.

'My word but I must have offended you mightily,' Frank drawled.

'Not at all, but during your absence I developed expensive tastes,' she said sweetly.

'And long may you hold them!' His eyes glinted as he reached for her hand and kissed the back of it.

Despite herself Tansy laughed.

'So!' Frank leaned back slightly to taste the champagne.

'You are going to tell me that I'm interfering in what doesn't concern me,' she said.

'Not meaning that at all!' he protested. 'Tansy, you are the kind of person to whom anybody in trouble is inevitably drawn and you are also possessed of the liveliest bump of curiosity of anyone I know!'

'When I see someone in obvious distress I do feel obliged to listen when they confide in me,' she admitted.

'Well, we shall see if – ah!' He broke off as a gentleman who had just handed his cloak to a waiter paused on the way to his table.

'Cartwright, isn't it? I thought I knew the face! Celebrating your latest series of articles designed to appeal to the public?' the newcomer enquired.

'It's a living,' Frank said easily. 'Mr Henry Oakley is a publisher, Tansy. Miss Tansy Clark is a friend of mine.'

Henry Oakley was younger and more handsome than she had envisaged.

He bowed.

'Delighted to make your acquaintance, Miss Clark.'

'Will you join us?' Tansy asked.

'Break up a tête à tête? Cartwright would scarcely thank me for that though your offer is appreciated, ma'am,' Oakley said.

'It's not a tête à tête,' Tansy said bluntly. 'We were hoping to see you here this evening.'

'For five minutes then. Waiter! Hold my table, will you?' He drew up a chair and sat down, fixing keen dark eyes upon her. 'What can I do for you? You have written a book and hope to persuade me to read it?'

'Indeed I haven't!' Tansy said. 'If I had I'd've sent it to you in the usual way.'

'Then you would be unusual,' he said, smiling slightly. 'I must tell you, Miss Clark, that many would-be authors go to extreme lengths to arrange for me to read their manuscripts, being under the firm impression that I never trouble to read my post! What they fail to realize is that the only recommendation needed is a well-written piece of work that falls within our area of interest.'

'Philosophy and theology,' Tansy said.

'My late father's twin passions. They made him one of the most respected publishers in London, though, since his tastes were erudite, not one of the most profitable. So if you haven't written a book. . . ?'

'Have you recently entertained a young man called John Simpson to dinner?' Frank enquired.

'Simpson? The name sounds vaguely familiar but I haven't dined out for about a fortnight.'

'He offered you a manuscript and you invited him to dine with you?'

'Recently?' Oakley knitted his brows. 'Believe me, profits aren't so vast that we can afford to entertain authors indiscriminately! Yet the name – Simpson – Simpson – Lord, yes! I do remember!'

'He sent you a manuscript?' Tansy said eagerly.

'He brought it to the office. Respectable young man, late twenties, I'd say. He insisted on seeing me personally and I agreed to read his manuscript mainly to get rid of him.'

'When was this?' Frank asked.

'A few days ago – last week sometime.'

'Did you read the book?' Tansy asked.

'I did indeed – perhaps skimmed through it would be a more accurate description. It wasn't our type of book. In fact I would have been at a loss as to where to advise him to place it. A weakly plotted and quite badly written treatise on the joys of matrimony. I cannot imagine why he offered it to me in the first place!'

'Did you send it back to him?'

'That's our usual practice but he had neglected to put his address on it. He came back for it.'

'When?' Tansy leaned forward eagerly.

'Yesterday morning as a matter of fact. I didn't see him myself but my secretary gave him the manuscript back, together, I'm sure, with the usual soothing words designed to assuage hurt pride.'

'You sound judgemental,' Tansy said.

'Publishing is a business but we like to keep the flow of polite rejections as painless as possible. I had enclosed a short note with the manuscript wishing him better fortune elsewhere. I doubt if he'll get it.'

'Poor John Simpson!' Tansy sipped her wine and took a forkful of salmon.

'I am sorry to have disappointed anyone, especially if he is a friend of yours,' Oakley said, looking uncomfortable.

'I've never met him,' Tansy said, 'and neither has Frank. He and his wife rent a house near me and she hasn't seen him since yesterday morning. She told me that he'd gone to see you and thought he might have been invited to dine.'

'And he still hasn't arrived home?' Oakley looked from one to the other.

'I saw her again and he hadn't returned home.'

'How did he take the rejection?' Frank asked.

'I didn't see him of course, but my secretary said he took back the manuscript quietly, murmured his thanks and left.'

'And didn't go home.' Tansy frowned.

'Went somewhere to drown his sorrows I daresay,' Oakley said, rising. 'You'll probably find he's sleeping it off somewhere. I'd better claim my table!'

'His wife is exceedingly worried,' Tansy said.

'When did you speak to her last?'

'This morning actually.'

'Then depend upon it but he is likely to be at home by now. I am sorry if the rejection caused him distress but publishing is a business and not, unfortunately, a charity.'

There was a slight impatience in his voice.

'Thank you anyway,' Frank said.

'You're very welcome. Shall we meet at billiards in a week or two? If I recall you owe me a game.'

'Of course,' Frank said.

'I am delighted to have met you, Miss Clark.' Oakley bowed as he turned away and moved towards the other side of the restaurant.

'You didn't mention that you hadn't seen her since this morning,' Frank reproached.

'You think he will have been home in the meantime?'

'I think it might have been a good idea to check before you set off on your investigations.'

'Verity Simpson would have come to tell me if he had,' Tansy said obstinately.

'Not if he'd arrived half-intoxicated or in a foul temper. And he may have returned while you were at your father's.'

'You're very logical,' Tansy said crossly. 'I have a strong feeling that John Simpson has not yet returned home!'

'Eat your salmon,' Frank said with a glint in his eye. 'Fish improves the capability of the brain to think in sequence, I'm told.'

Tansy opened her mouth to reply and laughed instead.

'You know that my feelings are often acute and accurate!' she exclaimed.

'And your heart is wider than your waist. Eat your fish!' His hand briefly covered hers, averting an argument.

Obediently she ate and drank.

'Cheese or dessert?' Frank asked.

'Just coffee, please.'

Frank signalled to the waiter and the coffee was brought.

'Verity Simpson told me that her husband was often anxious and depressed. You don't think—?'

'I think it's far too early to think anything,' Frank told her firmly. 'Henry Oakley is probably right. Mr Simpson went off to drown his sorrows and will turn up in due course having convinced himself that Oakley cannot recognize a masterpiece when he sees one. Tansy, why do you constantly fret about other people's needs and neglect your own?'

'I look to my own needs very sufficiently,' she retorted.

'All of them?'

It was the nearest he had ever come to making a risqué remark. She drank her coffee hastily, aware that she was blushing, aware too that his eyes were on her.

'I shall go round to The Larches first thing in the morning and hope to meet John Simpson for myself,' she said. 'It was good of you to bring me here this evening, Frank. I appreciate it.'

'It was also for the pleasure of your company.'

'And we are good friends still though we argue a great deal?' She spoke lightly, the colour ebbing and flowing in her face.

'If best friends cannot argue,' Frank said, 'then who can?'

'Indeed!'

'So how shall we spend the rest of the evening?' he asked. 'As good friends, of course!'

'Would you think me very rude if I asked you to put me in a cab and send me home?' Tansy ventured.

'That was a brief best friendship!' he mocked.

'On the contrary, I am concurring with your opinion. Verity Simpson may well have left a message for me to let me know that her husband is come home and she has been fretting for nothing.'

'Would she do that?'

'I am sure she would. She was very glad to talk to me, for she finds the city very lonely – not that one can call Chelsea the city – but we are slow to take to strangers. She has ladylike manners, too.'

'Pretty, is she?' He flashed her a mischievious glance.

'Pretty and clearly devoted to her husband,' Tansy said.

'Then we must hope he has returned. I ought to escort you home.'

'And then come traipsing out to town again? I shall take myself home, and hope to receive good news. Pa will have to be told the news, whatever it is. He will be a mite disappointed if there is no problem for him to solve!'

'Shall I see you tomorrow?' Frank enquired as they left the restaurant.

'I've no plans.'

'Then I'll call round during the day. By then you will have learned that John Simpson arrived home safely – with a very bad headache – and we can talk of other matters.'

'I am always glad to hear details of your newspaper commissions,' she said demurely.

'Yes, I know you are.' He hesitated for an instant as if he was about to say something else, then hailed a dawdling cab and handed her up into it.

Pa would like us to make a match of it, Tansy thought as the cab began to move off, but Frank is just a friend.

The possibility that their friendship might grow into something more was something she had occasionally considered.

Frank was attractive, earned a good if irregular salary, took an interest in her welfare, sought her company, sometimes seemed on the verge of saying something more but never did.

And her own feelings? She liked him immensely but she had loved Geoffrey. Even ten years after his death that love remained. He had provided for her handsomely, left her the means to live as an independent woman.

Had loved? The phrase reverberated in her mind and when she briefly closed her eyes she found that, as usual, she couldn't summon up Geoffrey's face in detail.

THREE

The cab was making slow progress through the crowded streets. Tansy, opening her eyes and sitting upright, leaned to lower the cab window in the hope of relieving the stuffiness within.

The pavements were a moving stream of people walking past the shops, pausing to admire the goods on display in the new, modern plate-glass windows or hurrying towards the theatres whose billboards flared into brightness under the new electric lamps that had been installed.

Tansy, leaning her elbow on the narrow ledge as the cab went round a corner, repressed a smile as a woman in a bright orange jacket over a skirt that ended short of her ankles, clutched at her hat which was in danger of being tugged from her improbably vivid head by a gust of warm wind.

A tangle of horses just ahead was being sorted out, with their respective drivers loudly blaming the others for incompetence and bad driving. Her own cab was drawn up sharply to wait for a clear space. Oh for the peace of Chelsea! Tansy thought, involuntarily smiling into the face of a man thrusting his way past, bending to avoid a swinging street sign. Above the sign a lamp haloed him in gold and threw his features into sharp relief. Then he was gone, plunging past her into the crowds as her cab began to move ahead.

'Mr Simpson? John Simpson!' Tansy's voice was drowned in the rattling of wheels and the neighing of the horses.

The face into which she had looked had been the face of the groom in the wedding photograph that Verity Simpson had shown her.

'John Simpson!'

Sticking her head out of the window she shouted as loudly as she could and was assailed by catcalls and whistles from a couple of men who, having obviously dined rather too well, were supporting each other along the pavement. Biting her lip she hastily withdrew her head, wound up the window and sank back into her seat.

At least John Simpson was unhurt and either on his way home or, having been home, in town again, possibly hoping to track down Henry Oakley and beg him to look again at the manuscript. Whatever the circumstances his wife would be delighted.

Tansy relaxed, feeling suddenly rather foolish. Perhaps she was dwindling into one of those middle-aged single women who spent too much time looking into the affairs of their neighbours!

When she alighted at her gate she lingered to breathe in the fragrance of the stocks.

The front door opened and Tilde, dark curls framing her face, came out, a shawl round her slender shoulders.

'Mrs Timothy asks if you're coming in, miss,' she asked.

'Adding – "Or is she going to stand dreaming in the garden until midnight?" no doubt?' Tansy said, stepping into the hall.

'She frets about you, miss,' Tilde informed her. 'Did you find your father well?'

'My . . .? Oh yes, very well. Of course he cannot move without help but apart from that he is in excellent health.'

'I sometimes wonder where my father is now,' Tilde confided. 'Ma told me once he'd died – probably fighting a duel, for he was a French gentleman – at least they met in France – and they fight duels every day over there, don't they?'

'Do they indeed?' Tansy took off her hat and jacket.

'So Ma said. That must be how she knew that he was a nobleman, I daresay,' Tilde said. 'Noble people fight more duels than anyone else, don't they?'

'They probably do,' Tansy said solemnly. 'You and Mrs Timothy may go to bed now if you wish. I'll lock up.'

'Mrs Timothy went already, miss,' Tilde informed her. 'At least, she's taken off her corsets on account of her back is breaking though as we know she never complains about it!'

Mistress and maid exchanged smiles and Tansy went into her sitting-room where the long curtains had been drawn against the darkness.

'Did you want a nice cup of tea, miss?' Tilde was at the door, hesitating.

'If I do I can make it myself. Was there something else?'

'Mrs Timothy was saying earlier as there's a couple of very good music halls in town,' Tilde said.

'There are indeed.'

'It seems a shame,' Tilde said wistfully, 'that a woman like Mrs Timothy who works all the hours God sends never gets to go to the music hall. Don't you think so, Miss Tansy?'

'I do indeed!' Tansy composed her face to solemnity. 'It has been on my mind for some time that neither Mrs Timothy nor yourself get to go anywhere. The music hall sounds like a splendid idea. If you and Mrs Timothy wish to go I shall be happy to bear the expense, and you may choose your own evening. Now, good-night!'

'Thank you, miss!'

Her mission accomplished, Tilde dropped a curtsy and withdrew.

Tansy pulled back one of the curtains and unlocked the french window, stepping through on to the terrace, raising her arms to take out the pins that confined her thick red hair.

Geoffrey had teased her about her hair, telling her that in some countries red hair was considered a blemish and people made a sign against the evil eye when they saw it. Geoffrey had never reached out to take the pins from her hair and feel its luxuriant weight for himself.

She shook her head at her own foolishness and went down the steps and across the lawn, where flower-borders gleamed whitely in the dark and the river splashed beyond the low wall.

It was tempting to slip over the wall and walk along to The Larches where, she suspected, Verity Simpson still waited for her husband to return, unless somehow or other he had contrived to hire a cab and was already there. Better not! John Simpson had been in a hurry but he hadn't seemed to be seeking transport.

'It is,' she thought chidingly, 'none of your business, Tansy Clark,' and she turned, walked back into the house, where she locked the french windows carefully and closed the curtains, more for Mrs Timothy's peace of mind than her own.

She went through the small house, dimming the lamps, and into her bedroom which held, ironically, the large double bed she and Geoffrey had chosen together, she in her early twenties and rather embarrassed when the shopkeeper invited her to sit down on the mattress, as Geoffrey, some years older, sandy haired, pleasant-voiced looked on.

'If anything happens to me,' he had told her on the day of their parting, 'the house and furnishings are yours.'

'Nothing is going to happen to you! Why should it?' Tansy had said crossly. 'You are not going into wild parts to be attacked and eaten by savages!'

'No indeed, but the islands of the Caribbean can be more treacherous than they appear, and in order to study the native artefacts it will be necessary to go quite deeply into the jungle.'

'Then you must take a good supply of quinine and take care of snakes,' Tansy had instructed.

'My dear, I always do and when you travel with me all my precautions will be doubly careful,' he had promised.

She never had travelled with him. Neither hostile natives nor snakes had ended her dreams of married life, but yellow fever, his brief illness and death, the news being conveyed via the Consulate. Since then she had lived contentedly enough in the house with the furniture they had chosen together, had used the annuity he had left her wisely, had filled the bookcases with the novels she enjoyed reading, unconsciously relegating Geoffrey's thick tomes on archaeology and native art to a lower shelf.

Now as she brushed her hair the unbidden thought came that if she ever married anyone else she would sell the bed and buy another. It was a thought that smacked of treachery and she swiftly quelled it, got between the covers and extinguished the lamp.

Next morning, reminding herself that Frank had mentioned

he would call, she she put on a light-blue dress with ruffles at neck and hem, then took it off again and substituted a dark skirt and high-collared white top, coiling her hair severely at the back of her head. A glance in the mirror showed her a tall, slim, businesslike young woman with no frilly concessions to femininity. Tansy made a face at herself, sprayed a light jasmine perfume – a Christmas gift from Frank – behind her ears and went downstairs, resolving to stop shilly-shallying.

'You look ever so smart this morning, miss!' Tilde said as she brought in the toast and coffee. 'Are you expecting Mr Frank to call?'

'He might call in,' Tansy said casually.

'Ah!' Tilde sent a meaning look and vanished kitchenwards.

Tansy, chewing her toast, resolved to conduct herself in future with such dignity that Tilde's pert tongue would be stilled. On the other hand the girl meant no harm and it was pleasant to know that one's servants had one's best interests at heart!

'Did you mention to Mrs Timothy about the proposed trip to the music hall?' she asked when Tilde came in with fresh coffee.

'Not yet, miss. I'll tell her when she gets back.'

'Gets back from where?' Tansy enquired, faintly surprised.

'She went up the road just before you came down for breakfast, miss.'

'Why did Mrs Timothy go up the road? If her back is still hurting I would go and instruct the doctor to come here to see her.'

'She never mentioned her back, miss,' Tilde said.

'What took her out?'

'There's quite a crowd of people up there,' Tilde said chattily. 'Mrs Timothy told me to bring your breakfast and went off to see what was going on. You're not annoyed, are you, miss?'

'Of course not. Mrs Timothy arranges her own times. It is only rather unusual.'

'It's been promising rain too,' Tilde said, adding virtuously: 'I reminded her to take her brolly.'

'That was sensible of you. Thank you, Tilde. You can clear away now. I'll just finish my coffee.'

The sound of the back door opening and closing and the slap-slap of Mrs Timothy's umbrella as she shook it over the sink announced the housekeeper's return.

'Mrs Timothy, what on earth took you out so early?' Tansy stepped across to the large cheerful kitchen where a fire burned even at the height of summer.

'The butcher's boy came by early, Miss Tansy, which is a most surprising thing in itself,' Mrs Timothy said. 'That lad must need to be pulled out of bed every morning for you can get no sense out of him until midday! If you'd seen the tongue he tried to palm off on me last week – well, it'd shake your faith in human nature, miss!'

'Never mind the tongue,' Tansy said impatiently.

'Oh, the crowd, yes. Well, the butcher's boy said as there was a bit of a stir further along the road so I grabbed my brolly and went up to see if there was anything I could do.'

'And?'

'There wasn't much to be seen,' Mrs Timothy said with regret.

'What was to be seen?' Tansy spoke with forced patience, knowing from past experience it was almost impossible to hurry up her housekeeper when the latter had information to impart.

'Just the crowd, miss, and a policeman. The milkman was there and fortunately I'm on good terms with him since we do order quite a lot of cream. The young gentleman from The Larches got himself drowned.'

'Drowned?' Tansy stared at her.

'Drowned dead so the milkman said,' Mrs Timothy said. 'They found him on the water wheel this morning. Tied himself to it, he did, and then drowned, the milkman said. One of the men in the crowd said that he actually saw the corpse and his face was all bruised and swollen. Gave him a very nasty turn!'

'But this is awful,' Tansy said numbly.

'It's terribly awful, Miss Tansy!' Mrs Timothy said with a certain grim relish. 'It would have turned my insides to jelly if I'd seen it I can tell you!'

'You didn't . . . ?'

'No, miss. The policeman was keeping people from the back of the house. Such a sad affair! His wife went out early this morning on to the towpath and saw him as the wheel turned, so the milkman said.'

'His wife found him?' Tilde clasped her hands tightly together. 'That's exceedingly tragical!'

'She ran to the cab-stand and one of the cabmen came back with her while another fetched the police and the doctor. It wasn't no use. He was stone dead.'

'It must have been a dreadful shock for the poor young lady!' Tilde said.

'Indeed it was, my dear. The milkman had turned up by then and he said he could hear her sobbing something pitiful.'

It was becoming painfully clear what had happened. Tansy felt a pang of real guilt. If only she'd had the presence of mind to jump out of the cab the previous evening and insist on talking to John Simpson! He had been obviously so shattered by the rejection of his manuscript that he had wandered about in a distraught state and finally, overcome by depression, had gone home and drowned himself.

'Is Mrs Simpson sure that the body is that of her husband?' she asked on a sudden thought. 'After drowning . . .'

'Bruised and swollen!' Mrs Timothy nodded mournfully.

'Shall I get you a drop of brandy, Mrs Timothy?' Tilde asked solicitously.

'Just tea, dear, with plenty of sugar – and perhaps a tiny drop of medicinal brandy,' Mrs Timothy accepted.

'About the deceased . . . ?' Tansy said.

'Well, bruised and swollen it may well have been and indeed I've no reason to doubt the milkman. Indeed I've always found him most reliable and obliging. It was Mr Simpson, miss, because he was still wearing his wedding ring. It seems they each had a ring with their names engraved on the inside – his name in her ring and her name in his ring.'

'That's very sad and romantic,' Tilde said, pouring the tea.

'They'd only been wedded about a year,' Mrs Timothy said, taking a noisy gulp. 'Poor young lady! She seemed so lost when I spoke to her the other day – lonely and forlorn. And she's a religious woman too, for she was quite upset at not being able to find the church.'

'I could have prevented this!' Tansy spoke tensely, her hands clenched.

'I don't see how, miss,' Mrs Timothy said, after another gulp of her tea.

'I saw him last evening,' Tansy said.

'I didn't know as how you knew Mr Simpson, miss,' Tilde said.

'Not personally, but I knew what he looked like. Last night I glimpsed him and – if I'd only followed—'

'You wouldn't've been following the right gentleman, Miss Tansy,' Mrs Timothy broke in. 'The doctor told the milkman that the poor young gentleman had been dead for two days.'

FOUR

Tansy's first instinct had been to rush round to The Larches and check the details of the drowning for herself but her commonsense told her that it was wiser to wait. By midday the crowd would have drifted away and she could then call upon the unfortunate Verity Simpson. Meanwhile she forced herself to sit at her desk and check the household accounts, a task she'd been delaying because it was so mind-numbingly mundane. As she jotted up the columns of figures, her thoughts insisted upon revolving about the man she had seen from the cab the previous evening.

'Now, Tansy, take a quick careful look at every third person we see and then you can describe them for me when we get home.'

Thus Pa, before his injury, playing the 'noticing game' on one of their walks together.

'And the next person we saw?'

'A man with a cap on and dirty boots.'

'And what was between the cap and the boots?'

'He was thin and his shoulders were a bit bent, Pa.'

'So what kind of man was he?'

'A poor man?'

'And probably suffering from a chest complaint which makes him hunch his shoulders in that manner. Very good!'

'Really, Laurence,' had complained her mother with a smile, 'anyone hearing you would think you were training the child to be a detective!'

'It doesn't hurt anybody to have sharp eyes and a good memory,' Pa had said. 'Anyway it's good fun.'

It had also been useful. Tansy rather prided herself on the fact that she not only seldom forgot a face but could usually place it in its setting.

Tansy had lunched on a cup of soup and a sandwich, neither Mrs Timothy nor Tilde being in any state to provide anything more substantial! From the kitchen came the sound of eager speculation with Mrs Timothy regaling Tilde with accounts of other spectacular drownings she had heard about, read about or occasionally witnessed.

Tansy put on her dark jacket and straw hat, which were surely sober enough for the occasion, left the house and walked up the road. The crowd had, as she had expected, drifted away and she went up the short path and rang the bell. The least she could do was offer her sympathy.

The door was opened very slowly. Through the narrow gap Verity Simpson's voice issued tremulously.

'Miss Clark? Oh, I thought it was another one of those policemen or a dreadful newspaper reporter. Do please come in!'

She opened the door sufficiently wide to allow Tansy to enter and immediately shut it again, turning a pale, piteous face to her visitor.

'I was very sorry indeed to hear the news,' Tansy said. 'It must have come as the most terrible shock.'

Verity Simpson clutched at her hand.

'All last night,' she said, 'I kept hoping he would come home. This morning I decided that I would wait for a couple of hours and then go to the police station. He would never have stayed away for two nights, indeed he would not! Then I wondered if he had returned but instead of entering the house taken a long walk. He often does – did that when he was depressed. He never wished to trouble me with his moods.'

'How did—?'

'This morning – I hardly slept all night – I rose and dressed and went down through the back garden to the river bank. The bench down there, near the water wheel – he liked to sit there and watch the river. The wheel was turning as it always does and I saw . . .'

She uttered a little choking sound.

'It must have been dreadful for you,' Tansy said.

Verity Simpson nodded miserably.

'Have you eaten today?' Tansy looked at the frail figure.

'Eaten?' The other dabbed at her eyes with the sodden handkerchief she was holding. 'No, not yet. I just stood there. I couldn't believe what I was looking at and then a man who'd been fishing further along the bank must have seen it too and he came running up. He went to fetch a policeman and after that – I had to identify him. His face – they said he'd tied one hand to the spokes of the wheel and been dragged down as it continued to turn.'

'That sounds unlikely,' Tansy said doubtfully.

'He was always very clever with his hands,' Verity said. 'He had once thought of joining the merchant navy but then he became very interesting in writing and met me and – we have only been married a year, Miss Clark!'

She dissolved into racking sobs.

'Come into the breakfast room and I'll make some tea – do you have any in the house?' Tansy enquired comfortingly.

'I still haven't bought any milk,' Verity said, dabbing still at her eyes. 'Someone said the milkman was here but – I wasn't really paying attention.'

'Coffee then? I'll make us some coffee,' Tansy said, guiding Verity into the small gloomy room where she had drunk coffee before. 'You sit down and I'll get it brewed.'

At least the fire was alight and a kettle on the hob showed signs of boiling. Tansy took off her hat and busied herself with making the coffee. Verity, slumped in a chair, looked smaller and more fragile than ever.

'Drink that.' Tansy handed her a cup of black, heavily sweetened coffee. 'Have you any relatives who could come?'

'Only an elderly aunt in the Midlands and she hasn't seen me for years.'

'But if you write to her she might offer support?'

'I don't think so. My parents never liked her very much so they rarely met. When they died she did send her condolences but that was all.'

'It seems rather unfeeling,' Tansy commented.

'She's been an invalid for years, I believe, so one couldn't have expected her to travel to the funeral,' Verity said.

'And your husband? Hadn't he any relatives?'

'Some distant ones I think.' Verity sipped her coffee, a trace of colour returning to her face. 'He broke with them some years ago. They disapproved of his literary ambitions and urged him to settle to a steady job. I've never met them.'

Tansy grimaced slightly. An impecunious young widow with no family or friends was in an impossible situation unless she had resolve and toughness of character – qualities in which the fair, delicate girl in the chair opposite was sadly lacking.

'You must consult a lawyer,' she said at last. 'He'd be in a better position to advise you. Your husband must've left some provision for you?'

'John hadn't any money at all,' Verity said, putting her cup shakily on the table. 'We used my dowry to marry on and for lodgings and then we moved here and rented this house. It was paid for three months in advance and I've sufficient to live on for several weeks.'

'And after that?'

'I shall get a job,' Verity said.

Now wasn't the time to ask her what job she thought she could do, Tansy reflected. It was highly likely that she'd been educated like a lady by parents who'd left her very little.

'Forgive my asking,' she said after a moment, 'but you are sure the body was that of your husband?'

'There's no doubt,' Verity said sadly. 'His face was – very badly battered but he was wearing John's clothes and – I think I told you about our rings – his was on his finger with my name inside.'

'I'm so sorry,' Tansy said gently. 'If there's anything I can do . . . ?'

'The police said there would have to be an inquest,' Verity said. 'I wonder if you . . .'

'I'll be glad to accompany you,' Tansy said promptly.

'Thank you. I couldn't bear to go there alone.'

'I daresay it'll be quite straightforward,' Tansy assured her. 'If you're in need of some company now . . .'

'It's very kind of you, Miss Clark.' The other drew a deep breath and made an ineffectual attempt to tidy her straying curls with her fingers. 'The truth is that I must get used to the idea that John won't be coming home – he won't be coming home ever again. At the moment it seems like a bad dream but it's real and I have to accustom myself. I think I need a little time in which to – adjust. Of course there will be the funeral to arrange. Oh, I hope they will allow a church service in view of what seems to have happened. John cannot have been entirely in his right mind when he – but it won't do to dwell on these things. I just feel so tired.'

She looked exhausted, dark shadows under her eyes, her fingers trembling as they plucked aimlessly at her skirt.

'Why not have a good long sleep?' Tansy suggested. 'I shall tell my maidservant to bring round some groceries later on. She can make up the fires for you as well.'

'If it wouldn't be an imposition . . . ?'

'Tilde's a handy little soul. Is there anything else?'

'The vicar – ought one to see the vicar?'

'I can send a note round to him if you like,' Tansy offered. 'He's very sympathetic.'

'We are not regular communicants but I do like to go as often as I can.'

Verity managed a weak and watery smile.

'And when you've rested,' Tansy said, rising, 'it might not hurt to write to your aunt and tell her what's happened. People whom you think of as generally unsympathetic can often surprise you in times of trouble. Get a good sleep first. Tilde will be along later. No, don't get up. I can see myself out. Again, please accept my condolences.'

She patted Verity on the shoulder and went out into the passage leading to the front hall. As she closed the door she heard Verity begin to cry softly again.

The doors of the other rooms stood open. On impulse Tansy stepped into the front room and took up the framed photograph that lay on the table there. It was the portrait of the Simpsons on their wedding day.

Looking down at it she frowned uneasily. There was no doubt in her mind that the man in the photograph was the same man she had seen the previous night as her cab had been stuck in the traffic tangle. Her memory had obviously played her false but she still found it almost impossible to believe. This was the man she had seen. She knew perfectly well that it couldn't've been but she was sure that it was.

Turning the photograph over she saw the name of the photographer's studio stamped in ink on the back. M. Curry. Regent Street.

After a moment's thought she put the photograph down again and let herself out quietly through the front door.

Tilde was in the kitchen, polishing silver with a dreaming expression on her face. She looked up as Tansy came in.

'Mrs Timothy went for a lie-down,' she volunteered. 'She was quite shook up after this morning.'

'This afternoon I want you to take some groceries round to The Larches,' Tansy said. 'You know the house?'

'I've passed by it, miss. Why do—'

'Mrs Simpson will need to eat,' Tansy said briskly. 'She won't feel like cooking though. Take some bread, some butter and milk – a jar of paste – have we eggs?'

'Yes, miss, and some boiled ham.'

'Those will do very nicely – and some tea. Put it in the small canister. And perhaps a couple of apples. Go round about three or three-thirty.'

'I'm sure that if my poor husband drowned himself dead I'd never eat again!' Tilde said.

'You would you know. Grief is blunted after a time and then one feels like a good meal,' Tansy told her.

'Well, until I get a husband I won't know how I'll feel when he's drowned dead or killed in a duel,' Tilde said sadly.

Tansy bit back a chuckle and went into the sitting–room. Seated at her desk she took out paper and pencil and wrote the name 'John Simpson' on the page.

It was such an ordinary name, probably shared by hundreds of men all over the country. A young man who was good-looking enough to be noticed but not handsome enough to excite envy. No family? Most people had family somewhere or other. Perhaps, since he had literary ambitions, he had been ashamed of his low beginnings, fought for an education, weighed up the possibilities of a naval career, decided to try to make his mark as a writer. Was that why he'd married Verity? She had no parents to interfere and a reasonable dowry to start off their life together until he had achieved publication.

She was getting cynical, Tansy decided, decorating the name with curls and squiggles. Verity was young, slim, fair and pretty. Any man whether he needed money or not, had every right to fall in love with her.

Yet the man who loved her had waded out into the river, tied his wrist to the slow-moving wheel and drowned himself. Had the brusque rejection of the manuscript so crushed his spirit that he'd had no heart to carry on living?

It had happened the day before last apparently. In that case he had killed himself only hours after he had been told his book wasn't wanted. But why had he come back here to this quiet corner of Chelsea in order to end his life? He'd been in the centre of London! He could have bought laudanum, checked into an hotel, slept his last sleep there. Instead he'd returned to the tranquil riverbank behind the house he had rented with his wife and made certain not only that he would be killed but also that his body would be quickly found and identified. Had that been his way of ensuring that his wife was not left too long in suspense before she knew where he was, or had there been some other reason?

Impatiently Tansy screwed up the paper, tossed it into the wastepaper basket under the desk and stood up. A small mirror on the wall reflected her worried face and severe bodice.

There was no need to go round looking as if she personally was in mourning, she decided, going upstairs and yanking open her wardrobe door. The ruffled skirt and blouse of pale lilac, the former stretched over a small bustle, were light and summery without being too bright.

'That looks lovely, Miss Tansy!' Tilde said admiringly as her mistress arrived in the hall. 'Is Mr Frank coming?'

'No indeed! At least – it's possible he may call in,' Tansy said. 'If he does tell him that I've gone to my father's house.'

'Yes, miss. It's close on four. Shall I take the groceries to The Larches now?'

'Yes, please. Ah, Mrs Timothy, I thought you were resting!' Tansy spoke in smiling surprise as her housekeeper appeared on the stairs.

'Recovering from the shock,' Mrs Timothy said, descending

with her usual dignity. 'My nerves aren't what they used to be, Miss Tansy. Was the day when I could've stood any number of corpses fished out of the river but age tells!'

'You never said you saw the corpse,' Tilde interjected.

'I didn't. But my imagination supplied the details and that was quite enough to upset me,' Mrs Timothy said. 'When you are older you will understand the problem of combining a bad back with shattered nerves, not that I complain! And where are you going?'

Tansy hastily explained.

'Very kind of you to think of that, Miss Tansy. Had I been more in command of my nerves I would have suggested it myself! Go along then, Tilde, and if the poor young lady requires any further help then please give it to her, and be respectful now and don't go worritting her with any of your frenchified words!'

'Yes, Mrs Timothy.' Tilde took her leave.

'She's coming on very nicely,' Mrs Timothy observed.

'Thanks to your supervision,' Tansy said gracefully.

'She's a taking little thing when all's said and done,' the housekeeper allowed. 'Will you be dining in?'

'I'm going to Pa's house. I shall eat there.'

'And if Mr Frank calls?'

'Then tell him where I am. I will see you later on.'

Tansy took her leave, conscious of the older woman's slight smile. Her servants, she thought, as she walked briskly to the cab-stand, were altogether too interested in her private affairs and she guessed that when she was elsewhere and the kitchen door firmly closed their talk must often turn to whether she would ever marry.

'Not until Fr – someone asks me and probably not ever!' she thought now, hastening her pace and waving down a cab.

The early-evening editions of the newspapers were just being cried in the streets as they entered the city.

MAN DROWNED ON CHELSEA WATER WHEEL
GROTESQUE SUICIDE IN CHELSEA

The headlines screamed at her. Tansy rapped on the cab roof and bought a paper.

Considering the incident had occurred early that morning the actual information gleaned had been scanty.

> A young gentleman, recently arrived in Chelsea and married for only a year, was this morning found dead tied to a water wheel in the Chelsea reaches of the Thames. He had been absent but not reported missing for two days and was discovered by his wife, Mrs Verity Simpson while she was taking an early stroll along the riverbank.
>
> Hearing her cries of shock and distress a gentleman who was fishing on the riverbank nearby but not within direct sight of the water wheel, ran to help her and seeing the ghastly sight ran to the nearest cab-stand and requested assistance.

Tansy alit at her father's house, paid the cabby and hurried up the steps just as Finn opened the door.

'You've 'eard then, miss,' he said, his gloomy face hiding delight. 'Is it the gentleman you've mentioned was missing?'

'Apparently there's no mistake. You've had the newspaper, then?'

'Not fifteen minutes back, Miss Tansy. Your pa's still reading it.'

Tansy went up the staircase into the large sitting-room and was greeted by her father who looked up from his newspaper and said,

'It looks as if your neighbour couldn't face rejection.'

'Does it mention his being a writer in your newspaper?'

'Not a word! The standards of journalism and detection are definitely falling these days – apart from Frank's pieces, of course. He came by earlier and I packed him off to the morgue to see what else he could discover.'

'I just missed him, then!' She felt an unwarranted stab of disappointment.

'He took a cab and said he'd be back directly. I doubt if at this stage he'll glean much more in the way of information.'

'Did he tell you about last night?'

'Started to and then we heard the newspaper sellers start up their caterwauling. Are you staying for dinner or is Frank whisking you off somewhere expensive?'

'I can't answer for Frank but I shall eat here if that isn't going to put Finn out,' Tansy said.

'Nothing you ever did, Miss Tansy, could put me out,' Finn said from the doorway. 'I take it that Mr Frank will be eating here too?'

'I am sure he will. He will be bowled over by Tansy's lilac outfit,' Laurence said.

'He will be staying because he wants to discuss the most recent events and for Finn's cuisine,' Tansy contradicted.

'I'll put on a couple of extra chops,' Finn said. 'If he's on his way from the morgue he'll be hungry!'

'Visiting a morgue would have the opposite effect on me,' Tansy said, taking off her hat and jacket.

'Aye, they are sad, bleak places,' Laurence agreed. 'When I witnessed my first autopsy I felt very sick though happily I didn't pass out cold as any corpse on the floor as my colleague did! But nobody enjoys a visit there.'

'Did Frank tell you about last night when we met Mr Henry Oakley?' Tansy seated herself.

'He was launched on his narrative when the newspapers criers began their cacophany. Tell me yourself – and pour us both a glass of wine first. I am cutting down on the whisky. Too heating in the summer!'

FIVE

'So the young man's manuscript was rejected, eh? That must have been unpleasant for him but whether it would drive anyone to kill themselves is difficult to say,' Laurence said thoughtfully.

'If he had set his heart on it and was depressed – his wife did mention that he had moods and used to take long walks so as not to harass her with his own ill-humours.'

'You derived the impression that you were speaking to a wife who was genuinely happy with her husband?'

'Very much so. Pa, you don't like that wine! For heaven's sake give in to temptation and let me pour you a whisky!'

'A very small one,' Laurence said.

Tansy did the honours, conscious that she had more to tell but not wishing to start until Frank had arrived.

A few minutes later footsteps on the staircase announced him and he came in looking cheerful.

'From the look on your face there's news to tell,' Tansy said.

'And a mystery already bubbling away! Was that roast pork I smelled as I passed the kitchen? I'm starving!'

'If I visited a morgue I wouldn't eat for a week,' Tansy told him.

'That's due to your feminine sensibilities, girl. You look very nice this evening!'

'You don't have to sound so surprised,' Tansy said, taking her place at the table.

The meal as usual was delicious. Finn's culinary skills far outclassed his criminal expertise though he had given up the latter years before.

When they had finished and the dishes had been cleared Finn brought in the coffee and a decanter of port and joined them as he usually did.

'What did you find out at the morgue?' Tansy asked.

'Exactly what I expected to find.' Frank passed along her coffee. 'I know the attendant who's on duty this week so it was a simple matter to get to view the body. The doctor had already drafted his report. Male in his late twenties. Middle height. Fair hair. Face quite badly damaged and swollen. Left wrist deeply incised by rope burns. He'd quite obviously tied himself to the spokes of the water wheel.'

'While it was still moving?' Laurence questioned.

'The wheel turns very slowly,' Tansy said.

'And an athletic man with the rope already around his wrist could've reached out and secured the other end to the spokes. Mind you he'd have to work hard!'

'John Simpson originally wanted to go to sea,' Tansy said. 'His wife told me. Probably he knew about knots and things like that.'

'You've seen her again?' Frank looked at her.

'I didn't rush in the moment I heard what had occurred,' she answered with spirit. 'I waited until lunch-time when the crowd had drifted away. She was still very upset – deeply shocked by what had happened. I sent Tilde round with a basket of groceries and told her to offer what help she could to Mrs Simpson who isn't the most efficient housekeeper.'

'Hardly likely to be when she's just heard of her husband's suicide,' Laurence said.

'Actually saw the body on the water wheel,' Tansy reminded him. 'You're right, of course. She was very anxious about his not coming home when I first met her but she hasn't done anything to spruce up the place and if he had arrived safe and sound there was no milk for his coffee.'

'When you saw her today did you tell her that we had spoken to Henry Oakley?'

'No, I didn't! She must have realized by now that his death may have had something to do with his writing.'

'She didn't say so?' Laurence sipped his port.

Tansy shook her head.

'She just kept crying and saying he was subject to fits of depression. I managed to calm her down a little and persuaded her to go and rest for a couple of hours.'

'Once the rejection of his book is made known at the inquest a motive for killing himself will have been established,' Laurence said.

'Would someone actually kill themselves because they couldn't get their work into print?' Tansy wondered.

'Chatterton did.'

'Pa! Chatterton wasn't married and he was an opium-addict! And that was more than a hundred years ago anyway!'

'Seems a rum way to top 'imself,' Finn mused.

'Meaning?'

'If he was in London proper already why not jump into the river there? Why go all the way 'ome and wade out into the water and pick a slower death?'

'Quicker than you might think. The wheel spokes would've crushed him fairly fast.'

'Pa! that's a dreadful way to die!'

'Exactly!' Finn nodded solemnly. 'Most coves what top themselves picks an easier way – overdose of opium or quick jump from a high place. He must've been in a bad way!'

'How was he dressed?' Laurence enquired.

'Very neatly. Black-and-white striped waistcoat, black trousers, dark-blue jacket. No hat or gloves or shoes.'

'Frank.' Tansy set down her cup. 'Did the morgue attendant say how long he'd been dead?'

'About forty-eight hours. You know it's hard to be exact in these matters?'

'Why?' Laurence asked, giving her a sharp glance.

'Last night after I left you,' Tansy said, 'I saw John Simpson.'

Three pairs of eyes were fixed upon her.

'But you never met him,' Frank said at last.

'I saw his photograph when Verity Simpson asked me in for a cup of coffee yesterday morning. She showed it to me. A study of the two of them on their wedding day. I saw the same man last night from the cab a few minutes after Frank had left me.'

'It was dark,' Frank objected.

'There was a traffic snarl-up just ahead as we turned the corner into the side street. The cab had to stop for a minute or so and I let down the window because it was stuffy inside. He was coming towards me along the pavement and he paused for a moment under a lighted sign. I saw him clearly.'

'Then you must have been mistaken,' Frank said.

'Tansy has an excellent visual memory,' Laurence said. 'I trained her myself! Remember our game, Tansy?'

'You bred a habit in me, Pa. I still take notice of what people look like.'

'But surely . . .' Frank looked at her.

'When I heard that he'd been dead for two days I thought that I must have been mistaken too,' Tansy said, 'so when I went over at lunch time to see Verity Simpson I sneaked another look at the photograph. It was the same man I saw last night in the street.'

'Then he cannot have died two days ago,' Laurence said. 'He was found early this morning which means he must only have been dead for less than twelve hours.'

'I put Tansy in a cab at about ten,' Frank said.

'And I saw him in the street less than five minutes later!'

Laurence said, hand cupping his chin: 'If Tansy saw John Simpson last night around ten then he can't have been dead for more than about eight hours when he was found. I find it hard to credit that such a mistake could have been made.'

'Then Verity Simpson must have made a mistake when she identified the body,' Tansy argued. 'Poor girl! She will be relieved to —'

'Don't rush to tell her that she made a mistake,' her father warned quickly. 'It may yet prove to be her husband.'

'The police seem quite satisfied,' Frank said.

'So what now?' Tansy demanded. 'Are you discounting what I saw?'

'Not in the least, but even being sure that you've seen some one after they've apparently committed suicide isn't evidence. Have you arranged to see Mrs Simpson again?'

'I feel somewhat obliged to keep an eye on her,' she admitted. 'She has no relatives beyond an aged aunt she hasn't seen for years, and her husband had no family at all. I shall go with her to the inquest if she wishes.'

'And beyond that for the moment there's nothing to be done.'

'I've some work to catch up on,' Frank said. 'May I see you home?'

'Very well, thank you.' Tansy affected not to notice the pleased look on her father's face. 'If I see John Simpson again I assume that I ought to follow him?'

'Not without great caution!' Laurence frowned at her. 'By now word of his death is in most of the newspapers. If there's been a genuine mistake he'll come forward of his own accord. If not – kindly remember you're the only daughter I've got!'

'I'll remember, Pa. 'Night, Finn!'

She put on her hat and jacket and went ahead of Frank down the stairs.

'You're pretty certain it was John Simpson you saw, aren't you?' Frank said as they walked towards the cab-stand.

'I'm absolutely sure!'

'Then I'm willing to be convinced. I wonder who did drown himself!'

'I'm wondering how a man can drown himself on a water wheel and not be found for two days when the wheel's constantly turning.'

'The riverbank is hardly the main highway,' Frank demurred.

'I know. We get the occasional fisherman there,' she allowed. 'But, Frank, I've walked along that path twice in the last couple of days and I actually noticed the wheel turning. There was nobody tied to it.'

'He could scarcely have committed suicide and tied himself on later!' Frank objected.

'Could he have got tangled up in a length of rope?'

'The rope was tied properly round his wrist with the other end which was fairly short secured to the wheelspoke,' Frank told her. 'The morgue attendant said he had certainly drowned. His lungs were full of water. The damage to the face occurred after death – the action of the wheel and the water.'

'Ought we to say something?'

As they got into a vacant cab she looked uneasily at him.

'The fact that you didn't see a body on the wheel and that you thought you glimpsed John Simpson in a crowded street after he'd actually killed himself isn't evidence,' he said. 'If you had a witness now . . . ?'

'I shall take care to provide myself with one next time!' she retorted sharply. 'Frank, ought not Henry Oakley to be told?'

'That a rejected author killed himself in a fit of despair? Rather hard on the poor man!' Frank sounded wryly amused. 'Anyway he will almost certainly have heard the news by now. The rejection might provide a motive for the suicide in which case he may be needed at the inquest. You know I've just thought of something!'

'What?' In the half-light she turned her face eagerly towards him.

'That you must be the only woman in the world with whom I'd share a hackney cab for the pleasure of talking about sudden death.'

'And what,' she enquired drily, 'would you usually be doing?'

'This.'

His hands cupped her face and his lips were warm. For a moment she let herself relax into his embrace and then drew away slightly.

'Now you're not going to object to a kiss between friends, are you?' Frank asked, a smile in his voice as he leaned back.

'I ought not to have asked such a question,' Tansy said, torn between pleasure and embarrassment.

'You know you can ask me anything, Tansy girl.' The smile in his voice was warmer. His hand reached to cover her own.

'Then I must take care not to ask improper questions in the future,' she said, embarrassment triumphing.

'And there's no time to persuade you otherwise for we are coming into Chelsea,' he said.

'Are you coming in for a drink – coffee?' she asked when they stood on the pavement.

'Not tonight,' he said. 'I have a mind to wander over to White's. Henry Oakley is a member of that club and I shall be interested to observe his reaction to the news of John Simpson's death.'

'Perhaps he will offer to do something for Verity Simpson,' Tansy said.

'For conscience sake? Tansy girl, you don't know much about publishers, do you? They are businessmen, not charitable institutions. I shall see you soon.'

He kissed her cheek and climbed back into the cab.

Tansy stood for a moment until her flushed cheeks cooled before she went up the path and her heart was unaccountably light as she fitted her key into the lock.

'Did you have a pleasant evening, Miss Tansy?' Mrs Timothy enquired, bustling forward to take her jacket and hat.

'Very pleasant, yes.'

'Your pa is in reasonable health and good spirits?'

Mrs Timothy had never actually met him but she never failed to enquire.

'In very good health and spirits. Of course Finn looks after him very well.'

'He always sounds to me like a most superior servant!' Mrs Timothy said.

'We must take care,' her father had joked more than once, 'that your Mrs Timothy and my man Finn never meet or there may be a fine romance for them and the necessity of finding new staff for you and me.'

'Pa and I are both fortunate in our household staff,' she said now.

'And myself in my employer,' Mrs Timothy said with a graciousness worthy of the Queen. 'I understand you are not averse to our visiting the music hall one evening? It is a long time since I had the pleasure of joining in the good old songs – and really, miss, some of the artistes who perform there are quite refined these days.'

'Just let me know when you'd like to go. Where's Tilde?'

'I sent her off to bed with a nice cup of tea,' Mrs Timothy informed her. 'The poor child took the groceries round for Mrs Simpson but when she got to the house everything was topsy-turvy and so neglected that she felt obliged to stay and help – not a lamp well trimmed and the fire smoking and the poor young lady rooting in a wardrobe trying to find a black dress! Tilde did everything she could to make the place more comfortable and she was really wearied when she got back!'

'Verity Simpson is the helpless kind,' Tansy said. 'You go on up, Mrs Timothy. I'll finish locking up.'

'In my opinion that poor Mrs Simpson requires a good hard-working servant-girl,' the other said. 'I'm very sorry that her poor husband drowned but if you ask my opinion it was very selfish of him to go off and kill himself and leave his wife without help in the house!'

'I don't suppose that he was thinking about that kind of thing at the time,' Tansy said.

'And why take a large house and expect his wife to do all the work in it I should like to know!' Mrs Timothy sniffed loudly. 'Too proud to get a proper job if you ask me! Will you be wanting anything?'

'Nothing, thank you. I hope your back is better?'

'As to that,' the housekeeper said with a heavy sigh, 'I never complain as you know, Miss Tansy, but ever since I heard the news about Mr Simpson its been acting up something cruel! Good night, miss!' She moved majestically away.

Tansy, going into the sitting-room, thought wryly: 'If I ever marry I shall be on tenterhooks until Mrs Timothy has bestowed her approval!'

But she was never going to marry anybody, she reminded herself. That first flush of love never bloomed twice and a woman was a fool if she went seeking it! An even bigger fool if she allowed herself to think of a man who was still sowing his wild oats and whose job kept him away almost as often and as long as Geoffrey's job had done!

She blew out the lamp and went up to bed, telling herself that from now on she would concentrate firmly on the puzzle that the recent death had presented.

The morning brought blue sky and a warm breeze that exiled from her mind the odd disjointed dreams which had disturbed her sleep. She had been in a cab and someone had seized her and embraced her but when she opened her eyes she saw the drowned, bloated face of a stranger and when she struggled free and tried to open the window, to lean out and call for help, she had seen only mocking faces flashing past as the vehicle gathered speed and she realized with horror that it was no longer a cab but a water wheel with herself trapped inside and the water beyond the spokes rising to cover her mouth and her nose . . . .

She had woken with a jump, pushing back the blanket which had crept too high about her neck, and sat up, wincing at her own childish terror at what had been no more than a nightmare already breaking up into jagged pieces and falling through the meshes of her mind.

'You look a mite peaky, Miss Tansy,' Tilde said when Tansy came down for breakfast.

'I slept heavily,' Tansy said. 'Mrs Timothy said you were a great help to Mrs Simpson yesterday and quite tired yourself out.'

'The hearth hadn't been cleaned for days,' Tilde said in so neat an impersonation of Mrs Timothy that Tansy wanted to laugh.

'Well, you did very well,' she said approvingly.

'There's one thing about me, Miss Tansy,' Tilde said with a touch of pride, 'I don't mind setting my hand to anything and making a good job of it even if my father was a French aristocrat!'

It was fortunate that she bobbed out of the room at that since Tansy, her eyes downcast, might have hurt her feelings very much by laughing!

Having finished her breakfast she put on her straw hat, charmed Mrs Timothy out of a bottle of wine and a large portion of layer-cake and set off for The Larches. Perhaps if she took one more look at the wedding photograph she would discover that her memory had been at fault though secretly she doubted it!

Verity Simpson opened the door, wearing a black dress that drained whatever colour was left in her cheeks.

'I hope I've not disturbed you but I brought round some wine and cake in case my maid hadn't . . .' She proferred the basket.

'Wine and cake? How kind!' Verity summoned sufficient animation to open the door wider and stand aside. 'Do please come in, Miss Clark.'

'Thank you and it's Tansy. Miss Clark makes me feel like a schoolmistress.'

Tansy stepped over the threshhold.

'And I am Verity,' the other said with the ghost of a pale smile.

'Verity.' Tansy acknowledged the informality with a slight bow.

'Please come through.'

Verity preceded her into the small gloomy room where an unwashed coffee-cup on the table lent weight to Tilde's low opinion of Mrs Simpson's housekeeping skills.

'Tilde was helpful, I hope?' she said aloud.

'Oh yes, most willing. It was very kind of you to send her over and the groceries were . . . I must owe you for—'

'Not at all. You were welcome,' Tansy said.

'The police came earlier,' Verity told her, taking a chair and motioning her visitor to another one. 'Oh, I must offer you coffee – tea?'

'Nothing, thank you. The police came . . . ?'

'A police officer,' Verity said. 'The inquest is to be next Friday. I shall be very glad to have it over!'

'I think that it will probably be a mere formality since nobody actually saw anything,' Tansy reassure her.

'The police officer told me that death was due to drowning and to the damage inflicted by the spokes of the water wheel. I can't bear to contemplate . . .' She pressed her lips tightly together and swallowed convulsively.

'I'm sure he was very considerate,' Tansy murmured.

'Yes. Yes, he was very kind. He asked me if John was subject to melancholy and I had to admit that he was! You know he really thought his book would be accepted but it appears that Mr Henry Oakley rejected it. One cannot blame him of course but if only . . .'

'Yes,' Tansy said gently.

'He originally hoped to join the merchant navy, you know, but he could hardly swim at all! It was a disappointment to him at the time but then he met me and discovered that he had a gift for writing and . . .'

'Have you written to your aunt yet?' Tansy asked, fearing another bout of weeping.

'I intend to write to her,' Verity said. 'They told me that I may hold the funeral on Tuesday. The vicar—'

'My apologies! I forgot to contact him,' Tansy broke in.

'There was no need. He had heard the news and was kind enough to send round a note to me. I have attended service on a few occasions, though I regret to say that John was not of a religious inclination.'

'Will your aunt come to the funeral, do you think?'

'It's very unlikely,' Verity said. 'She is actually my great-aunt and she is very old indeed. In her sixties I think.'

She made it sound as if her aunt was in her dotage, Tansy thought. She felt a fresh stab of pity. Verity couldn't be more than three-and-twenty and seemed in most respects to be much younger.

'I must go,' she said aloud. 'If you need anything. . . ?'

'You've been very kind. People are being very kind,' Verity told her. 'Another neighbour has called and will help me with the funeral arrangements. But I must begin to contrive for myself. I always rather leaned on John you see. Now I must fend for myself.'

'There's no need to see me out,' Tansy began.

She wanted to take another swift look at the wedding photograph but Verity was obviously determined to be the polite hostess as she opened the door and ushered Tansy into the front hall again.

'Even Mr Henry Oakley sent round a messenger to express his sympathy at my loss and to tell me that John had called at his office and taken the manuscript away with him,' Verity was saying as she opened the front door.

Oakley might have taken the trouble to call round himself, Tansy mused, since it was surely unusual for a rejected author to commit suicide over the rejection.

She shook hands and walked down the short path to the street. In her imagination the figure of the drowned man dangling from the water wheel kept recurring, the more horrific because she hadn't actually seen it.

How could it have gone unnoticed for two days when she herself had walked twice along the riverbank, though admittedly she had scarcely glanced towards the water wheel? But Verity had been there – seated on the bench on the first occasion, hurrying through the back garden of her rented house on the second! John Simpson must have been still alive then.

Perhaps he'd been near on the first occasion, concealing himself until the riverbank was deserted. No, that wouldn't do either! The doctor had said the man had been dead for two days.

A new thought struck her so suddenly that she almost stumbled and then she had turned and was hurrying to the cab-stand.

SIX

'Good day, Miss Clark! Terrible about the suicide, don't you think?'

The cabby held open the door for her.

'Yes indeed.' Tansy nodded.

'Where to, miss?' He closed the door and prepared to mount up into his seat.

'Regent Street, please.'

'Ah, the ladies will have their shopping trips!' he said genially as he clambered aloft.

If only! Tansy thought wryly. She would have enjoyed a pleasant shopping trip with the prospect of replenishing her autumn wardrobe, but there were more pressing matters to attend to.

Suppose Verity had lied and the man in the photograph hadn't been her bridegroom at all? Tansy could think of no good reason why she should have lied but no avenue was too narrow not to be explored.

'Any particular shop, Miss Clark?' The cabby opened the trapdoor to enquire.

'Anywhere will do.'

With a driver who obviously relished a bit of a gossip with his passengers she had no intention of informing him she wanted the Curry Photographic Studio!

He dropped her off at the corner and she strolled along the street, pausing to admire some of the displays behind the plate-glass windows in some of the more modern establishments. Tricorne hats were very much in fashion this year, some trimmed with military braid, others decorated with small coloured feathers. Colours were darker and richer and figured materials much in evidence. Bustles were getting smaller which would make sitting down less cumbersome.

Michael Curry was embossed in curly golden letters over a recessed doorway. The bow-window at the side held several framed photographs of young ladies holding roses and small children with dimples. Tansy pushed open the door and heard the bell tinkle as she did so. The interior was a long room divided by red curtains, both held back to reveal an inner dais with a tall pot-plant and a chair draped with a variety of coloured shawls and scarves. A camera on a stand, both covered with a black cloth, loomed in the corner. The near space held a long counter with a till at one end, opposite which the wall served as a backdrop for more photographs, this time unframed.

'Yes, madam?'

A bespectacled young man materialized from within the curtains and approached her, bowing.

'Mr Curry?' Tansy enquired.

'His assistant, ma'am – Thomas Wilks at your service.'

'I am making enquiries concerning a wedding photograph,' Tansy informed him.

'We have our prices here and the various stage settings we

can provide in order to display your chosen pose in the best possible—'

'No, it is not for myself I enquire,' Tansy said. 'I am not here to make an appointment. I am making enquiries about a wedding photograph which has already been taken. I suppose Mr Curry keeps copies of the photographs he takes?'

'Only for a certain time, madam. He certainly retains copies of those he regards as particularly interesting and, with the written permission of the sitters, displays some in the window or on the wall. If there are any particular examples you would care to see?'

'About six months or a year ago a young couple had their wedding photograph taken by Mr Curry – a Mr and Mrs John Simpson?'

'We get so many bridal couples,' Mr Wilks said. 'Mr Curry however is in the habit of retaining them for up to a year.'

'And there would be a record of the appointment and the pavment rendered?'

'I can certainly look, madam. Oh, please do take a seat!'

Tansy obediently perched on the high stool by the counter while the assistant dived behind to burrow in the cupboards that lined its other side.

'Simpson, Simpson!'

He had lifted a large and clearly heavy volume on to the counter and was leafing through it with aggravating slowness.

'Mr and Mrs John Simpson,' she prompted.

'Ah yes! Here we are! Would you care to see the results, madam? It looks very charming if I may venture to say? I do hope there are no complaints?'

He had carefully swivelled the volume round for her to see.

'No. No complaints.' Tansy looked closely at the picture. 'Yes, that is certainly them. The problem is – the gentleman is John Simpson, I assume?'

'He certainly said that he was!' Mr Wilks looked rather shocked. 'Yes, I recall that he addressed his wife as Verity. Rather a charming name, I thought.'

'Did he have any proof of his identity?'

'Proof, madam? Why would he give that name unless he were . . . ?'

'The world,' Tansy said gravely, 'can be a deceptive place.'

'Indeed, madam! Indeed it can,' the other returned fervidly, 'However Mr Curry refuses to photograph bridal couples here in the studio unless they bring a copy of the marriage-certificate with them. Now that may sound unusual but some years ago we had a couple who were not wedded at all but pretended to be for a wager.'

'Very shocking!' Tansy said.

'Indeed it was, madam. We live in very scandalous times as Mr Curry so often says,' he agreed.

'Would it be possible for me to see Mr Curry?' Tansy asked.

'You'd be welcome to see him, ma'am, but he seems to be away at the moment. Has been for several days. He does sometimes take a week off to visit his sister – he trained me personally in the use of the camera so if you wanted —'

'Not at the moment but certainly at some future stage. I am sorry to have taken up your time.'

'I hope the photographs were judged satisfactory?' he said with a touch of anxiety. 'Mr Curry prides himself on being a skilled and reputable photographer.'

'Yes, they were judged most satisfactory,' Tansy said, rising. 'You don't recall the couple yourself I suppose?'

'I cannot say that I recall the bride in any detail – one hardly likes to stare at young ladies.' Mr Wilks blushed slightly. 'I do flatter myself that I have a good memory for faces however! One moment!'

He bent behind the counter again and came up with a large accounts ledger.

'Simpson, Simpson – yes, of course. Two guineas paid for the framed photograph just over five months ago. Mr Simpson came in to pay it when Mr Curry was absent and I dealt with the matter. He was very pleased with the result and said his wife would be delighted.'

'He came in alone?'

'Yes he did.' Mr Wilks nodded. 'He looked a trifle shabby – not in the pink, so to speak.'

'Depressed?' Tansy ventured.

'Yes, that is the word I would have chosen. Rather unusual for a recently married man to be in dismal spirits but as my mother often says courtship can turn to disillusionment very swiftly! Not that he said anything in the least derogatory about his good lady! Indeed he did mention that they had just returned from a brief holiday – a honeymoon so to speak – *la lune de miel*, as the French say.'

'Do they indeed?' Tansy commented.

The mad idea of introducing him to Tilde brushed the edges of her mind and was quickly dismissed. She was too fond of her maid to expose her to the possibility of meeting Mr Wilks's mother!

'Of course he may have felt a trifle low at the prospect of returning to the workaday world,' Mr Wilks was chatting on, putting the ledger back in its place and coming round the end of the counter to open the door for her. 'And his wrist may have been hurting.'

'His wrist?'

'He'd sprained it trying to turn a boat too quickly. I recall it because he apologized for signing awkwardly with his right hand.'

'His left hand you mean.'

'His right hand, ma'am. Mr Simpson was left–handed.'

'But . . .' Tansy let the syllable die into the air.

John Simpson had tied his left wrist to the water wheel. That meant that he was right-handed, but this young man had just stated definitely that he was left-handed.

'You're sure you're not mistaken?' she pressed.

'Absolutely certain, ma'am.' Hesitating, he went on, 'I do apologize for asking but is there some difficulty associated with Mr John Simpson?'

'You've not heard?'

'Heard what?' he enquired.

'John Simpson was found drowned. It was in the newspapers.'

'I don't indulge in newspapers,' he said primly. 'What an awful . . . ! But he had returned safely from his boating holiday!'

'He was drowned in the Thames – in Chelsea.'

'I am very sorry to hear it!' He took off his spectacles, polished them carefully and put them on again. 'Was it an accident?'

'I don't know, Mr Wilks,' Tansy said uneasily. 'I really don't know!'

Leaving him shaking his head at her information she went out into the street again.

Her interest in the latest styles had evaporated. She hailed a cab and directed the cabby to drive her to the pleasant crescent where her father lived.

Twenty minutes later she was seated opposite Laurence with Finn hovering in the background while she rapidly told of her encounter.

'Was this Mr Wilks absolutely certain that John Simpson was left-handed?' Laurence demanded.

'Absolutely certain – those were his exact words. He said that when John Simpson came to collect the photograph and pay for it he signed for it very awkwardly with his right hand. He said he had hurt his left wrist turning a boat – a rowing-boat I suppose – during his honeymoon.'

'Trying to drown 'imself even then!' Finn commented.

'I don't think so,' Tansy said. 'He probably took his wife out on a river or a lake somewhere. He always wanted to go to sea.'

'She didn't mention to you whether he was right or left–handed?' Tansy shook her head.

'Maybe,' said Finn on a note of inspiration, 'he was ambi-, ambi- whatever.'

'Ambidextrous,' Laurence supplied. 'I doubt that since he would surely have mentioned the fact to the photographer's assistant when he told him about the accident. The point is that if he was left-handed he'd've tied his right wrist to the wheel.'

'Unless his wrist was still injured?' Tansy suggested.

'Not six months after it happened unless it had been badly broken – there was no mention of a broken wrist in the autopsy, was there?'

'No, nothing.'

'And if his wrist was still hurting,' Laurence continued, 'then one assumes he would have chosen a less bizarre method of doing away with himself. Tying his wrist to the wheel would have been a difficult enough feat with two perfectly uninjured hands. Tansy, I think the police should be informed! Shall I send Finn to request that the chief inspector call upon me?'

'If he didn't tie his wrist to the wheel,' Tansy said slowly, 'then perhaps – perhaps he didn't kill himself, Pa?'

'All we can say at this juncture is that his wrist was tied to the water wheel but he met his death by drowning,' her father said.

'I think we ought to 'old off for a bit before sending for the hinspector,' Finn said decidedly. 'If we're right we ought to get the credit of solving it all.'

'Finn displays a most regrettable quality of finesse on occasion,' Laurence said with a smile.

'Are you seeing Frank this evening?' Tansy asked.

'Am I seeing Frank?' Her father lifted an eyebrow in her direction. 'Usually that's my question to you, dear!'

'Oh, I never see him unless I now and then bump into him accidentally,' she said, rising casually and reaching for her hat.

'If you do see him,' Laurence said, 'then tell him the latest development. He may have a few bright notions.'

'A very bright gentleman is Mr Frank,' Finn said. 'Seems a crying shame to me he ain't got a wife to settle him down.'

'Frank Cartwright is not the settling-down type,' Tansy said firmly. ' 'Bye, Pa! I shall walk across the park to get a cab. It's a lovely afternoon.'

The small park opposite the crescent of houses provided a short cut to the cab-stand though this was something of a misnomer since few could resist lingering along the winding paths that wandered between flowering hedges with beds of annuals under the trees, benches set at intervals and a pool where children could sail their boats.

It was in the park that Geoffrey had proposed marriage to her. More than ten years ago, Tansy reflected, as she entered the gates. Would the day ever come when she entered here without remembering?

Today the park was crowded. Hoops were still in fashion, she noticed with amusement, as two small girls bowled them along the path with their nanny, all flying streamers on a white cap, panted along with a baby-carriage clamped to her fingers.

She paused for a moment to tuck the coverlets in more securely just as a large jagged stone, flung with some force from over the hedge, skimmed off the hood of the perambulator and fell on to the path.

'Oh my heavens!' The nursemaid gave a shriek of alarm.

'Are you all right?' Tansy, who had stood aside to allow the other to proceed, went quickly to her side. 'Is the baby all right?'

'No damage done, thank goodness!' The nanny was rather pale but rapidly regaining her composure. 'Children can be so unruly these days, can't they?'

'Yes,' Tansy said thoughtfully, stooping to pick up the stone. 'One could not apply that to your own charges though.'

'Thank you. They are very good children.' The nanny smiled and hurried after them.

The stone had come over a high hedge. Tansy, sensing that it was foolish to give chase to a silent attacker, nevertheless walked to the nearest gap in the thicket and stepped through to the other side.

Here the path was much narrower with a wide border of plants, which had recently been weeded, leaving spaces of bare soil between. Someone had stood on part of the border in order to throw the stone. When she looked closely she could see the half-print of a shoe dug quite deeply into the soil. Certainly too large for a child, she reasoned as she stood up again and looked round. At the beginning of the path where it converged with the path she herself had taken, the beginnings of a small rock garden, too tiny really to justify the name, displayed tiny star-flowers clinging to stones of various sizes. The jagged stone in her hand fitted into a space as neatly as a piece in a jigsaw puzzle. Tansy stood straight, trying to order her thoughts.

Had someone seen her enter the park and followed her, picked up the stone and taken the parallel path in the hope of hitting her as she walked along at the other side of the high hedge? He had taken the risk of seriously hurting someone else. Had the stone landed in the baby carriage there might have been a tragedy.

'Taken up gardening for the neighbourhood?'

The voice made her jump out of her skin. She controlled her cry of alarm and sent Frank, who had just reached the dividing of the paths, a furious glare.

'What are you doing here?' she queried.

'I've just come from your father's house,' he said, looking faintly surprised at her vehemence. 'I missed you by no more than a minute so I held back my information and came after you. In fact I've been chasing you all over the place for the past couple of hours!'

'Why?' she asked bluntly.

'Because I've some news and it's only fair that you should get it first. Actually I went to your house earlier but Mrs Timothy said you were out so I guessed you were at Laurence's place and came over.'

'It didn't take you two hours to get from my house to Pa's!'

'No, of course not. I paid a call on Verity Simpson in between. Come and sit down and I'll tell you about it.'

'Shall we go back to Pa's?'

'Finn said he was taking a nap. We can tell him later on!'

'Very well, then.'

She suffered herself to be escorted to a bench near the bandstand where on fine evenings local musicians entertained the people in the park.

'As you were coming into the park just now did you see anyone leaving?' she asked.

'Quite a number of people. Why?'

'No reason.' She would keep the episode of the stone-throwing to herself for the moment in order to avoid being lectured about taking risks by walking about by herself. 'Tell me your news!'

'John Simpson was left-handed, so it's highly unlikely that he tied himself to that wheel,' Frank said.

'You've been to the photographer's studio!'

'Which studio?'

'The one who took the wedding photograph of the Simpsons. His name was on the back of it. Michael Curry. Regent Street.'

'And?'

'He wasn't there but his assistant remembered John Simpson because he'd suffered a slight accident to his left wrist when he went to collect the photograph and he apologized for his bad writing when he signed for it with his right hand.'

'So the information was confirmed,' Frank said.

'Who told you of it?'

'Verity Simpson. I told you that I called upon her after I found out that you weren't in.'

'I'm surprised she talked to you. She doesn't strike me as a young woman who'd chatter to a reporter.'

'Its my fatal charm,' Frank said with a grin. 'Bowls 'em over every single time!'

'I can't say that I've noticed,' Tansy said with asperity. 'What exactly did she say to you?'

'Only that she didn't know how she was going to manage now he had gone, how upset he must have been after his book was rejected. She said his handwriting wasn't always very easy to read on account of his being left-handed and she hoped that hadn't weighed against his work with the publisher.'

'Did you tell her that you'd talked with Henry Oakley?'

'I thought it better not. Are you inviting me to come home with you?'

'It's the least I can do,' Tansy said, rising.

'Because you missed me before?'

'To spare the susceptibilities of all the females who need a respite from your fatal charm,' Tansy said drily, and exploded into a chuckle as Frank, ceremoniously offering his arm, winked at her.

SEVEN

'Ah, you caught up with her, sir?'

Mrs Timothy looked embarrassingly coy as she opened the door.

'Your mistress can be irritatingly elusive, ma'am,' Frank said with a grin, handing her his hat.

'Tilde's doing some mending for me. Keeps her mind off sudden death and suchlike. Shall I bring in some tea, miss?'

'Please. Did you have lunch, Frank?'

'I did, but a slice of toast with Gentleman's Relish might go down very nicely,' Frank told her. 'Are you over the shock of hearing the news yourself yet, Mrs Timothy?'

'Very kind of you to ask, sir!' She beamed at him. 'Very kind indeed. Yes, the shock did upset me a mite – went straight to my back though, as you know, I never complain about it. Still living by the river ought to accustom one to a drowning now and then.'

She went into the kitchen. Going into the sitting-room Tansy took off her hat and jacket and raised an eyebrow at her visitor. 'Frank, if you need to charm the ladies don't go wheedling your way into my housekeeper's favour,' she said. 'You'll make her as silly as Tilde sometimes is!'

'Mrs Timothy is a treasure and I'd steal her away if I didn't know she was devoted to you,' he said.

'You're incorrigible!' Smiling even as she shook her head she sat down and looked at him.

'I'm also puzzled.' He took the chair opposite her, stretching out his long legs. 'A man has his manuscript rejected having presumably expected it to be accepted for publication.'

'That was the impression he left with his wife.'

'I asked her if she'd read her husband's book but she said she hadn't, that he kept his writing very private.'

'And he only had one copy of it. She told me that too.' She broke off as Mrs Timothy came in with the tea and toast. Not until she'd left the room did Frank say:

'And there was no suicide note.'

'He's hardly likely to have written one just in case he felt like killing himself!' Tansy protested.

'True, but after his manuscript was handed back to him he had several hours in which to decide what he was going to do.'

'He was so mentally shattered that he – no, that won't do.' Tansy bit her lip thoughtfully.

'Because if he'd killed himself in a sudden fit of despair he would have done it very soon after his rejection – leapt off one of the bridges, swallowed a huge dose of laudanum, something like that.'

'Instead of which he took a cab home – or maybe walked back after dark, swam out – no, that makes less sense!'

'I've not been able to trace any other published work of his anywhere,' Frank said, sinking his teeth into his toast.

'If that was the only book he'd ever written and he had the one copy might he not have destroyed it before he – maybe he told his wife that he'd had work published before just to appear more eligible in her estimation?'

'For a wife who's been married for a year she seems to know surprisingly little about her husband,' Frank said. 'He has no living relatives and she has only a great-aunt who quarrelled with her parents. He wanted to go to sea but decided to be a writer instead.'

'It's as well that he never went to sea,' Tansy said, 'as he failed to turn round a rowing-boat without hurting his wrist!'

'Tansy, come and walk with me along the riverbank,' Frank said, rising.

Tansy swallowed her tea, grabbed her hat and went with him through the french windows and down the garden.

'Why are we walking here?' she enquired when they had stepped over the low wall. 'You've seen the river countless times before.'

'Not with a view to studying the spot where a man drowned himself.'

'I still think the man I saw from the cab window was John Simpson,' Tansy said obstinately. 'No, I don't *think* it was. I *know* that it was!'

They had almost reached the spot where the water wheel slowly turned.

'It would be possible to sit on the bench over there and not see – notice rather – a figure on the wheel,' Frank mused. 'The bench is turned slightly in the other direction. Even though it's turning slowly enough for a man to swim out and lash his wrist to it—'

'But John Simpson couldn't swim very well at all!' Tansy broke in. 'Verity told me that was one reason why he decided against going into the merchant navy! If he'd wanted to drown himself he could simply have jumped in the water.'

'Leaving his shoes on the bank. Why would he do that?' Frank said, rising.

'He wouldn't have done that!' Tansy spoke eagerly. 'He'd have kept his shoes on and filled his pockets with stones so that the extra weight would drag him under more speedily.'

'In any case his shoes weren't on the bank,' Frank reminded them both.

'He was wearing shoes when I saw him,' Tansy said.

'Was the man you saw – very well, let's assume it was John Simpson – was he carrying anything? A manuscript under his arm?'

'He wasn't carrying anything. Frank, it was John Simpson I saw! But how could it have been when he'd already been dead for twenty-four hours?'

'I had another word with the doctor earlier today. He's prepared to agree that the body might've been in the river for a shorter period. The damage done by the water wheel made it hard to establish a definite time of death but it was definitely by drowning.'

'So Verity made a mistake when she identified him?'

'He had on the engraved wedding ring with her name inside it and he was wearing the same clothes he'd worn when he left the house.'

'Without his shoes.'

'Exactly!'

'But somebody ought to have noticed him as the water wheel came round!'

'Mrs Simpson told me she'd come down a couple of times and sat for a few minutes on the bench. Then you walked along and you both got talking and – she cannot recall even looking at the wheel.'

'She was worried because her husband hadn't come home.'

'On the second occasion she saw the body hanging from the wheel: that was a frightful shock for her, I imagine.'

'For anybody.' Tansy spoke soberly as they retraced their steps along the bank.

'True, though I fancy you'd bear up better?'

'It depends,' she said wryly, 'who was tied to the wheel. Frank, other people walk along the bank here sometimes. And the upper windows of the houses overlook the river.'

'The bank curves slightly so the water wheel wouldn't be visible unless someone leaned out of the window and craned their necks. Anyway, see for yourself! The houses here have back gardens crowded with bushes and trees that obscure the view.'

'Not to mention the net curtains,' Tansy said with a grimace as they strolled along. 'Privacy is a two-edged sword! But people taking a walk along the path here would have seen—'

'Is there a regular procession of people out for a stroll?'

'No,' she admitted. 'An occasional courting couple and the odd fisherman.'

'Even if someone had noticed something,' Frank pointed out, 'not everybody is willing to get involved with a police matter. No, I begin to agree with you. It certainly wasn't suicide. If the man you saw—'

'It was John Simpson.'

'Then after you'd spotted him from the cab window he made up his mind to go home. Nobody's reported picking up a fare resembling his description by the by, so he possibly decided to clear his thoughts and walk, probably rehearsing in his mind what story he was going to give his wife.'

'And then?'

Frank paused with one foot up on the low wall that divided her own back garden from the path.

'He decided to walk home along the riverbank and then someone attacked him – someone who held him under the water until he drowned —'

'Why would anyone try to kill him?' Tansy interrupted. 'This is Chelsea, not the East End!'

'Robbery?'

'They stole his shoes?' she said disbelievingly. 'The manuscript? No, who'd want to steal a badly written book that wasn't going to be published anyway?'

'Perhaps he was carrying something else? They took it and then lashed him to the water wheel – which means they'd've had to tow him out to the water wheel and tie him to it – you needn't look at me like that, Tansy girl! I know my theory is full of holes.'

'Yawning chasms!' Tansy said. 'Robbers hit people over the head and then run off, surely? They don't hang around to stage a suicide scene. And if it was someone who'd planned it in advance then how would they know that he'd be returning the back way?'

'I haven't the faintest idea,' Frank said, putting an arm round her shoulders as they went into the garden. 'Perhaps more will come out at the inquest.'

'I told Verity that I'd accompany her there if it's necessary.'

'There's the funeral first,' he reminded her.

'Yes, of course. That's not until Tuesday – not long to go but she must look upon it with dread. Should I—?'

'Tell her that you saw her husband after he was supposed to have drowned? Why raise false hopes?'

'I suppose not,' she agreed reluctantly. 'Will the funeral have to be postponed if there are any doubts?'

'So far you and I are the ones with doubts and not an atom of proof to back them up.'

'I wonder if Verity Simpson's great-aunt will turn up for the funeral,' Tansy said, going back into the sitting-room. 'I advised her to write to her but whether or not she did—'

'She did write and asked your Tilde to post it for her. Her aunt's name is Caroline Elder and she lives in Derby.'

'How on earth do you know that?' Tansy sank into an armchair.

'I asked Mrs Simpson and she told me. I fancy that young Tilde will have taken note of the address too.'

'Tilde is like the cat,' Tansy said. 'She will be killed by curiosity!'

'Her husband will need to lead a virtuous life.'

'Oh no.' Tansy's eyes sparkled with mischief. 'That would bore her dreadfully! No, at the least Tilde must be matched with an international spy who is always going off on mysterious journeys.'

'And speaks French,' Frank supplied.

'And speaks French!' Tansy agreed. 'Oh, and he must be a great lover of poetry. Tilde is in the habit of reciting it as she goes about her work.'

'Did anyone ever tell you that you have an eccentric household?' he remarked.

'Of course! What other kind is there?' she retorted.

'Bachelor lodgings,' he returned. 'One day you must come and visit me in my rooms. You will find them dull indeed.'

'Then I'll not trouble coming,' Tansy said promptly. 'In any case it would be wildly improper of me to come unescorted – and please don't say that at my age it wouldn't signify!'

'I wouldn't dream of saying anything so tactless! One more thing – are you coming out to dinner with me tonight?'

'You have a new theory about the drowning?'

'I was hoping to talk about other subjects than murder and suicide.' He had turned and was suddenly holding her hands, his grey eyes intent on her face.

Tansy drew her breath in sharply. It would be so easy to accept, to allow him to take her to one of the intimate little restaurants where two people could eat and sip wine and talk without the danger of being interrupted. It would be so easy to put on her most becoming dress and for once accept his compliments without turning them off with a jest – for once feel herself to be the young, attractive woman her mirror insisted she was.

And after that he would add her, albeit unconsciously, to the long list of pretty girls he took out and flirted with and sooner or later forgot. It would place their friendship on an entirely different level.

'Another night,' she said at last. 'Will I see you at the funeral on Tuesday?'

'Of course. Verity Simpson said that you had been kind enough to offer to accompany her.'

'I could hardly allow her to go alone – unless her aunt turns up, of course.'

'If John Simpson wasn't the man tied to the water wheel he

may turn up there himself – walking and not coffinned.'

'Do you think he might?'

'I think it in the highest degree unlikely! Goodbye for the moment, Tansy.'

She smiled, trying not to wish that she hadn't refused his invitation to dinner. A long quiet evening and a long night stretched ahead. At the sitting-room door with his hand on the handle he paused to glance back at her.

'Why were you so scared when I met you in the park?' he asked.

'I was a little startled, that's all.'

'Tansy, lies don't sit lightly on your face. You were not merely startled – you were frightened. Why?'

'Oh, my nerves—'

'Are usually as sound as a bell! Come on, Tansy girl! You asked me if anyone had passed me as I was entering the park. Did someone follow you there?'

'I think it's possible.'

'What happened?' he asked sharply.

'Someone flung a large jagged stone from that little rockery they're making at the place where the two paths diverge. It almost hit a nursemaid wheeling a baby-carriage.'

'Children throw stones sometimes,' Frank said.

'Over a very high thick hedge? Anyway there was part of the print of a shoe on the soil – an adult shoe and the jagged stone fitted very neatly into a space in the rockery.'

'Could whoever threw it see you through the hedge?'

'It's far too dense at this time of year.' Tansy shook her head. 'I worked out that whoever followed me into the park took the other path and tried to gauge which point I'd reached by my footsteps on the other side of the hedge.'

'For the time being it might be a good idea for you to keep out of lonely places,' Frank said. 'Why didn't you tell me at once?'

'Because I knew exactly what you'd say if I did!' Tansy said, exasperated. ' "Don't go anywhere by yourself, Tansy! Stay by the fire and read a book like a good little mouse!", so I kept it to myself.'

'I never knew before,' he returned with a grin, 'that mice sat by the fire reading books!'

'You know exactly what I mean! I will take care but I refuse to behave like a shrinking female even if someone is anxious about my making enquiries into John Simpson's death,' she said stubbornly.

'The day you turn into a shrinking female is the day that I give up reporting and take holy orders,' Frank said. 'Will you be going over to see Laurence before the funeral or shall I tell him your latest discoveries?'

'I shall wait until after the funerals but you may tell him – about John Simpson being left-handed but not about the stone. I could be completely wrong about that.'

'One hopes so! I will see you soon.'

He lifted his hand in a casual salute and was gone.

EIGHT

The next day being Sunday she took herself off to church, alert for any sign of Verity but the slight, frail figure didn't occupy any of the pews. She was tempted to continue on to her father's house and spend an afternoon with him there talking over recent developements, noting the salient points but it occurred to her as she walked slowly to the main gate that Laurence often advised, during the early stages of a case, that it was an excellent idea to take a day or two doing something quite different.

'Problems lie beneath the surface of the mind. Delving for them is like trying to catch the tiny bones in a fish – better to forget about them and go back later when they can be pulled out more easily,' had been one of his precepts when he had been expounding on his methods of investigation.

Accordingly, after lunch Tansy put on gardening apron and gloves and went out into the back garden to deadhead the roses and clear the weeds that had sprung up. Unfortunately, digging and pruning kept the hands busy but didn't much occupy the mind. Despite her resolve the same questions kept on recurring.

The day after tomorrow a man would be buried under the

name of John Simpson. There was nothing to suggest that he wasn't John Simpson save that she had had a fleeting glimpse of the same man in a crowded street, about twenty-four hours after he was deemed to have killed himself. Yet the man on the water wheel had worn John Simpson's clothes and on his finger had been the engraved wedding ring. Yet he had tied the wrong wrist to the spoke; his shoes were missing, and so was his rejected book.

More damaging to her idea that it might not have been John Simpson who had drowned was that he had definitely been the bridegroom in the photograph.

She picked up the basket of weeds, carried them to the compost heap at the far end of the garden, resisted the temptation to step over the wall and take a stroll along the riverbank and went somewhat grumpily back to the house where she instructed Tilde to heat the boiler and, having indulged in a long warm bath and washed her hair, slipped on a loose robe and came down to read a novel she had borrowed recently from the library over a light supper.

The next day it rained, turning the rose petals sodden under a sullen sky.

'Going to be a sad day for the funeral tomorrow,' Mrs Timothy observed, bringing in toast and tea midway through the afternoon. 'I do say that a nice sunny day always gives the dear departed a good send-off, so to speak! Tilde gets a bit of a migraine when the rain's heavy so I sent her up to have a hot soak, relieves the headache sometimes.'

'You are very kind to Tilde,' Tansy said.

'Well, I don't believe in being harsh with young servants any more than you do!' Mrs Timothy said judiciously. 'Mind you, it's not hard to indulge her a bit now and then. She has very taking ways, does our Tilde!'

'It's being small and slender with it,' Tansy said with a grimace. 'I am too tall to excite the protective impulse.'

'A few inches smaller than Mr Frank I'd say,' Mrs Timothy said, raising her eyebrows in a meaningful way as she went out.

Tansy, who had spent the morning sorting out her chest of drawers and making a conscientious list of garments to be retained, garments to be put in the charity box and garments to be cut up for rags, finished her toast and took up her novel again, knowing as she read it that her mind was merely skimming over the surface.

By the next morning the rain had ceased and the pavements gleamed under a pale sun. Tansy had donned an elegant dress and jacket of black silk and confined her heavy hair under a snood of black lace, with the result, she decided gloomily, of robbing her face of all its colour and making her look taller and thinner than ever. Tilde however gave her an admiring look as she came downstairs.

'You look ever so tragical, miss!' she approved.

'One doesn't attend a funeral wearing a red hat and carrying a balloon,' Tansy told her, picking up the severely black umbrella which provided adequate if sombre cover when it rained. 'Is your migraine better?'

'Oh yes! Mrs Timothy was ever so kind,' Tilde said, coming to open the front door. 'Will you be in for lunch or will you be going to the funeral meal?'

'I have no idea but I'll be out anyway,' Tansy said, opening her umbrella to protect herself from the drops still splashing from the trees lining the road, and turning in the direction of The

Larches. As she went she was conscious of several pairs of inquisitive eyes following her progress from behind net curtains along the row of houses.

The hearse, with its black-plumed horses and its two mutes in their sombre suits and coal-black top hats, was already drawn up at the gate of The Larches and the carriage behind held one slender, veiled occupant.

'I'm not late, am I?' Tansy enquired, ascending the step and taking the vacant space within.

'Not in the least, Miss Clark – Tansy.' Verity sounded quite tremulous but calm. 'I wish to get through this ordeal quickly. John never liked funerals.'

'I don't suppose any of us likes them very much,' Tansy said. 'The red roses on the coffin are from you?'

'The undertaker kindly acquired them on my behalf. They are not too lavish? John so disliked empty show!'

'They look just right,' Tansy assured her, wondering whether she ought to have provided a floral tribute herself.

Verity gave a stifled sob and then sat bolt upright.

'I intend,' she said, 'to meet the occasion with quietness and dignity. One so dislikes showing one's feelings in public – but oh! it is very hard. Very hard indeed!'

There was a number of bystanders in the churchyard. Tansy glanced at them as she went in. John Simpson was unlikely to have attracted many mourners except his wife but there were always people who made a habit of attending obsequies. She glimpsed Frank's head among the small crowd and took a step towards him just as he shook his head slightly.

'Shall we go in?' Tansy asked.

Four gentlemen – she recognized the churchwarden and one

of the choristers – had joined the mutes and were shouldering the coffin into the church. Verity nodded, clinging to Tansy's arm as they passed into the church, some of those gathered outside straggling in behind.

The funeral service plodded its weary way. Tansy, who loathed the panoply of death, was relieved when the business was over, the vicar having managed to speak a flattering eulogy for a man he had never met. Outside in the churchyard she stood by, relieved that Verity was carrying out her small part with the quiet dignity she had set for herself. Once the first sod of earth had been spaded upon the coffin she turned away, her shoulders shaking momentarily.

'May I be of assistance, ladies?' Frank had joined them, his fair hair glistening with stray raindrops as he removed his hat.

'Mr Cartwright, may I introduce you to Miss Clark?' Verity said, controlling her emotion as she turned. 'He writes for the newspapers but I granted him an interview the other day and he was most courteous.'

'Miss Clark and I are a little acquainted already.' Frank bowed slightly. 'How are you, Miss Clark?'

'Very well, thank you.'

So he didn't want to advertise their close friendship. Tansy inclined her head gracefully.

'You have not, I take it, arranged any kind of funeral lunch?' Frank was enquiring of Verity.

'I never thought of it!' Behind her veil Verity's eyes widened. 'John and I knew hardly anyone in the district.'

'May I suggest that you have a quiet luncheon with me? Miss Clark too, of course!'

'Thank you very much,' Tansy thought crossly. 'I'm not sure I relish being an afterthought.'

Aloud she said cordially,

'It's very kind of you but I promised to visit my father. Is there anything more that I can do?'

'You've been very kind.' Verity took her hand. 'I had half-hoped that Aunt Caroline might come but I have received no word. A quiet luncheon would be most agreeable, Mr Cartwright.'

Tansy smiled and moved away, feeling more ruffled than she had expected to feel. Frank, of course, wanted leisure in which to find out more about the dead man. It wasn't Verity Simpson's fault that even in mourning she was distractingly pretty!

She left the churchyard and hailed the first cab that veered towards her, giving her father's address.

'Staying for lunch I hope?' Finn said, opening the front door. 'I've some nice cod with a lemon-and-butter sauce. Where's Mr Frank?'

'Frank and I don't go everywhere together, you know!' Tansy said sharply as she went up the stairs.

Laurence, scanning the columns of the morning newspaper, swung his wheelchair around as his daughter came in.

'For heaven's sake take off that morbid jacket and cap, child!' he greeted her. 'Black should only be worn by candlelight. With bare shoulders and a jewel sparkling.'

'Such an outfit might have scandalized the vicar,' Tansy said drily, slipping off the offending items. 'And it's a snood, Pa, not a cap.'

'Why should the vic . . . ? Good Lord, this morning was the funeral, wasn't it? It completely slipped my mind!'

'Old age creeping on, Pa?' She sent him a teasing glance.

'Galloping, dear, galloping! How did the event go?'

'Smoothly and quietly,' Tansy told him, seating herself. 'John Simpson was unknown so the people who came were merely newspaper readers. Verity Simpson conducted herself with dignity. Oh, Frank was there.'

'He called in last night. Will he be along for lunch?'

'He took Verity Simpson off to luncheon.'

'Did he so?' Laurence leaned back in his chair and looked at her.

'Oh, I was included in the invitation,' Tansy flushed slightly. 'I cried off because I thought you might enjoy my company.'

'And Frank will want to glean more information from Mrs Simpson.'

'He already talked to her with his reporter's hat on.'

'Sometimes people know things they are not conscious of knowing,' Laurence said. 'Frank told me about the business of the wrong hand being tied to the wheel. Why did you go off to the photographic studio?'

'It was the only lead I had. I wondered if the man in the photograph was really the bridegroom. It turned out that he was.'

'And yet the man who drowned tied his left hand to the spoke when he was left-handed.'

'So it wasn't John Simpson!'

'He had some use in his right hand. Frank said that you were told he signed for the photograph with his right hand.'

'Somewhat clumsily because he'd hurt his left wrist.'

'Which would have healed in the months since then! If in fact he ever hurt it at all?'

'You've lost me, Pa!'

'I believe I've lost myself at this point,' Laurence said with a grin. 'Ah! here comes the fish.'

'So fresh it nearly skipped up the stairs ahead of me!' Finn declared.

'And I did see John Simpson after he was supposed to have been drowned!' Tansy said obstinately when the meal had been served and they were enjoying its delicate flavour.

'You haven't reported that?'

'What would be the use?' Tansy shook her red head. 'One brief unwitnessed glimpse in a crowded street in lamplight? There is nothing in that which would have provided any evidence or any reason to delay the burial. Have you spoken to anyone from the force, Pa?'

'Not yet. I am sure that questions are still being asked but until murder is proved the general opinion must lean towards a rather odd suicide. The inquest should be interesting.'

He applied himself to his vegetables with an air of finality. At least Frank had said nothing about the jagged stone that had been thrown over the hedge in the park, Tansy thought as she took her leave later on in the afternoon.

Tansy, starting to walk along the road towards the cab-stand, changed her mind and headed for the park gates instead. What had occurred might have been a stray shot from some ill-disposed person who hated nursemaids. She loved the little park and had no intention of being denied the pleasure of walking through it.

Today the previous day's rain had freshened the plants and still sparkled on the trees. A park-keeper was industriously wiping the damp benches down and two elderly ladies, well wrapped against the slight breeze, paced the path decorously.

She reached the cab-stand without incident and took a ride back to Chelsea, congratulating herself on having overcome the very slight frisson of nerves she had felt during her passage across the park.

Tilde, her face craving information, opened the door for her. 'Was it very sad, Miss Tansy? Did the poor gentleman have many people attend his funeral?' she demanded.

'Several drawn there by curiosity. Is your migraine better?'

'Yes, quite gone,' Tilde said thankfully. 'I only get it once or twice a year. It's a sign of an artistic temperament you know!'

'Is it indeed?' Tansy nodded amiably to Mrs Timothy who was emerging from the kitchen.

'Was it a good lunch?' the latter enquired.

'Oh, there was no funeral meal. I went over to Pa's and ate there,' Tansy told her.

'No funeral meal?' Mrs Timothy looked shocked. 'Why, it isn't a proper send-off without ham salad and coffin-cake! What could the poor widow have been thinking?'

'Mr Simpson had no family and Mrs Simpson has only an invalid aunt who didn't make the journey. The other people there were strangers. Mr Cartwright kindly took her to lunch.'

'Did he now?' Mrs Timothy's plump face tightened slightly. 'Well, that's very kind of him I'm sure. Can I get you anything, miss?'

'I am going to change into something less dreary,' Tansy said.

Upstairs she took her time, changing into a dress of figured green silk with ruffles at elbows and hem. Shaking back her heavy fall of hair she combed it back into a loose knot and went downstairs, picking up her library book on the way.

Despite her efforts it again utterly failed to hold her interest. Time and again she put it down and listened, waiting for the ring of the door bell and Frank's cheerful voice greeting Tilde in the hall. That he would come and tell her anything he had gleaned from his lunch-time conversation it never entered her mind to doubt, but the afternoon crept into twilight and no doorbell rang.

The heroine in her novel was trapped in a swamp from which she would certainly be rescued by the darkly handsome hero. He at least made haste to be on the spot and didn't keep a woman hanging about waiting for him to arrive, Tansy thought, putting the book down and draping a light shawl about her shoulders before she opened the french windows and went out into the garden.

The rain had soaked the turf and weighed down the rose petals now scattered upon it. The sky was a soft lilac edged with pink and the breeze from the river was sharper. Summer was drawing very slowly, very surely to its end.

She walked down to the low wall and stepped over on to the riverbank. No couples strolled here and no fisherman sat patiently in the long grass as she walked along, seeing from the upper windows of the houses on her left lights springing up to be reflected on the surface of the water for a moment or two before the drawing of heavy curtains shut them from sight and rendered the river gloomy again.

In the half-light the slowly turning water wheel had a sinister aspect. As the spokes turned a last flare of sunset dyed the water that splashed from the iron spokes, turning each drop of moisture into blood.

A young man, left-handed, married for only a year, had come here, his rejected manuscript under his arm and taken off his shoes, then waded out into the river with a tough cord tied about his left hand, the other end of which he had tied securely to the spokes of the wheel with the right hand he had difficulty in using. It was just possible, she granted, if she had been mistaken in her sighting of him the following night, but what had he done with his shoes? Where was his manuscript? Had he thrown it into the fast-flowing water or disposed of it earlier? And how could any author destroy something laboured over lovingly if there was no copy? Henry Oakley wasn't the only publisher in London!

She looked towards the broken gate of The Larches and the weed-filled overgrown back garden beyond. What would Verity Simpson do when the rent already paid was used up and more money was needed if she wanted to stay there? What work could she do? Her husband had left her in a very difficult position.

No lights were visible from the back windows though some of the curtains were not fully closed. It looked as if the pretty widow was enjoying an exceedingly long lunch with Frank Cartwright, Tansy mused, and then, making a face at her own illogical feelings, she turned for home again.

NINE

She had expected Frank to call round the next day but the morning moved into afternoon with no visitors of any kind.

Having eaten a solitary lunch Tansy put on a light jacket and a straw hat trimmed with green ribbon and went out, leaving Tilde and Mrs Timothy to drink tea and pore over the account of the funeral in the morning paper.

She had half-intended going to her father's but, having secured a cab, found herself giving directions to Regent Street instead. As she entered the photographic studio Mr Wilks, the gold rims of his spectacles glittering, hurried from behind the counter to shake hands.

'Miss Clark, isn't it? How pleasant to see you again! If you wanted to speak to Mr Curry I'm afraid he has not yet returned.'

'Mr Wilks, have the police been to see you yet?' Tansy asked crisply.

'On Monday afternoon. They wished me to confirm that Mr Simpson was left-handed.'

'So Frank must've had a word with them after all,' she said.

'Frank?'

'Someone I know.' Someone who generally shares information and ideas with me but now seems to be going his own road.

'I ought not to have said that,' Mr Wilks said, biting his lip in an agitated way. 'He did ask me not to mention—'

'He was merely confirming what he had learned from you,' Tansy said.

'Which the police also wanted me to confirm. I am required to give evidence at the inquest. It is not an occasion to which I look forward with any pleasure. I have never been in a courtroom in my life!'

'Did they say when the inquest was to be?'

'They said that I would be informed. The shop may have to be closed for the day I suppose if Mr Curry is still absent. Studio! I must remember to call it studio – Mr Curry is most particular in these matters!'

'Mr Curry is a conscientious employer?'

'Most conscientious but also very fair. He does rest a great deal of confidence in me though my photographic skills cannot match his. Oh, do please sit down! I am forgetting my manners.'

'Does Mr Curry go away often and leave you in charge?' Tansy asked, taking the profferred chair.

'From time to time. He likes to visit exhibitions, to study techniques. However business is rather slow at present. Much competition from rivals. The art of the camera is becoming very popular and sophisticated.'

'Yes, I can imagine,' Tansy said. 'Mr Wilks, is there anything else you can tell me about Mr Simpson? Anything at all?'

To her disappointment he shook his head.

'The police have already asked me that,' he said apologetically. 'I would not have remembered him at all – I didn't take the actual photograph. Mr Curry sees to that unless he is absent and then if only a straightforward likeness is required I see to it, but most of my time is spent in the darkroom with the processing, et cetera. And as I told you I was here when Mr Simpson came to collect the photograph.'

'Having sprained his hand while dealing with a rowing-boat. He was definitely left-handed then?'

'So he told me and he certainly wrote his signature very awkwardly with his right hand. I do follow your concern. The body was tied by the left hand, was it not? It was mentioned in the newspaper. I do not usually buy newspapers. My dear mother believed that a great cause of depression was reading about the dreadful things that go on in the world but after your visit I must confess that I did purchase one.'

'And since John Simpson was left-handed his right wrist would have been tied to the spoke if he had committed suicide in that way.'

'I see the implication,' Mr Wilks said soberly. 'Yes, Miss Clark. It is a thought to ponder. But I am absolutely certain that he had an injured left hand and that that was the hand he normally used. I cannot alter that fact any more than I can provide him with large feet.'

'What did you say?' Tansy looked at him sharply.

'He had very small feet. If you were to look at the photograph again you would see that's so, though the feet themselves are partly hidden by the legs of the chair on which his bride was seated.'

'You noticed his feet?' Tansy said.

'Mr Curry has always impressed on me that clients like to be recognized,' Mr Wilks explained. 'The trick is to memorize one or two salient features about them. In John Simpson's case his left-handedness and his unusually small feet. Of course I didn't have to use the knowledge because he never came in here again.'

'Thank you, Mr Wilks. Thank you very much.' Tansy rose, holding out her hand. 'Shall I see you at the inquest? I intend going.'

'Yes. Yes, I shall have to go.'

He sounded unhappy as if giving evidence at an inquest might in some way injure his reputation.

At the door Tansy turned abruptly.

'Which salient features enabled you to recognize me?' she enquired.

'The red hair and the height, Miss Clark.'

'I thought so,' Tansy said resignedly and went to hail a passing cab.

Half an hour later she was seated in her father's sitting-room retailing her recent interview.

'You do see, don't you, Pa?' she finished.

'The reason the shoes were missing is that he had very small feet. So he could fit into Simpson's clothes but not his shoes, therefore it wasn't John Simpson who drowned?'

'You don't sound very sure,' Tansy complained.

'Tansy, the man on the water wheel was wearing John Simpson's clothes including his wedding ring. The fact that the shoes were missing might *suggest* that his own shoes would have been too small or too large! It is proof of nothing unless the shoes are found.'

'You think it was the real John Simpson?'

'The facts point to it.' Laurence ticked them off on his fingers. 'His own wife who was devoted to him identified his clothes and the wedding ring he was wearing. Now, as his face had been damaged we might think that she had made a mistake in identification, but a wife knows her husband. She doesn't rely only on physical characteristics. One has an instinct when one loves. He was wearing clothes with which she was familiar and the ring she had given him.'

'And the shoes?' she persisted.

'Since the missing shoes haven't been found we don't know if they fitted him or not. Unless those shoes are found they have no relevance.'

'So did the drowned man have large or small feet?'

'I have no idea,' Laurence said. 'Mrs Simpson identified him mainly from his clothes and the wedding ring. She was genuinely upset. The police told me they'd seldom seen anyone in such a pitiable state.'

'So you have talked to the police!'

'They called round this morning. I am still occasionally asked for my opinion on certain cases,' he said drily.

'And then they take the credit for your advice!'

'As I'm officially retired it doesn't trouble me in the least so you need not get indignant on my behalf.' He gave her an affectionate look. 'Apparently the authorities have checked into his background.'

'And?' Tansy leaned forward eagerly.

'An orphan,' said Laurence, 'reared by some kindly neighbours but he left to make his own way in the world. The neighbours have since died but others vouched for the few facts available. He worked in a shipyard for a time and talked of making a career in the navy but never did anything towards achieving his ambition. He drifted off a couple of years ago and didn't trouble to keep in touch. Oh, and he did try his hand at writing! Several editors have come forward to say they received short pieces from him but none was accepted.'

'Verity said that he had moods of depression.'

'So at a pinch it might have been suicide.'

'I don't believe that,' Tansy said. 'I think someone else killed him.'

'For what motive? He had no money, no regular job!'

'I don't know.' She shook her head impatiently.

'At least we can agree that he's dead.' Laurence drew on his pipe and puffed a cloud of smoke into the air. 'I can follow your line of reasoning, my dear, but nobody else has been reported missing and his wife made a positive identification. No, John Simpson is dead. I grant you that there are puzzling features about the case but people who commit suicide often behave in illogical ways. Desperation overwhelms them. Did Frank learn anything from his lunch with Verity Simpson?'

'I've no idea,' Tansy said frostily. 'Frank's lunch was clearly one that lasted into dinner-time and I've not seen him since.'

'I see.' Laurence regarded his daughter mockingly.

'See what?' Tansy asked.

'That Frank was probably smitten by her charms. You said that she's pretty?'

'Small and slim with fair ringlets,' Tansy said gloomily.

'You've no concerns then,' Laurence said casually. 'Frank likes pretty young women but when he chooses a life partner he'll pick out the best.'

'Heavens, who cares about Frank Cartwright's private life?' Tansy said lightly. 'I'd better get back. About the inquest – do you think I'll be called to give evidence?'

'You've no evidence to give,' her father said bluntly. 'One brief glimpse of a man whom you thought you recognized isn't solid evidence, my love, and your speculations about the size of his feet and the missing shoes are just speculation. Will you go to the inquest?'

'Probably.' She caught his eye and grinned reluctantly. 'Yes, of course I'll go. Verity Simpson may want to enlist me as a chaperon again! I'll probably see you on Friday.'

'Right! I shall have a little cogitation in the meantime.'

'You think my ideas are too far-fetched? John Simpson killed himself in a fit of despair and the loose ends aren't important?'

'Loose ends,' said Laurence, puffing on his pipe again, 'are always important.'

Tansy went downstairs, waved to Finn who was making pastry in the kitchen, and took a cab home, realizing with a stab of impatience as she climbed into the vehicle that she had avoided taking the short cut through the park.

Did she really imagine that whoever had flung the jagged stone before was lying in wait for her every time she visited her father? She had always prided herself on being tough-minded, on not yielding to feminine fears. She stopped the cab at the corner of her own street, paid off the driver, and walked with deliberate slowness past the houses, each one with its small patch of garden, its gleaming white step and its bow-window with the obligatory lace curtains. It occurred to her now as it had before that behind every quiet, respectable façade must rage the most violent emotions of love and hate and every emotion in between. If all that emotion was transformed into steam the roofs would fly off!

She had reached The Larches and paused for a moment to look at the patch of grass with its uncut rose bushes and the heavy drapes drawn together behind the bow-window. Either Verity thought that her windows should be shrouded for some days after the funeral or she simply hadn't troubled to draw them – or was she out somewhere?

Tansy gave herself a mental shake and walked on, telling herself that what John Simpson's widow did with her time was no concern of hers. After a bereavement many people wanted to sink out of sight for a long time and neighbours ought to have the tact to stay away.

Mrs Timothy had seen her coming and opened the door.

'Mr Cartwright called.' She stood aside as Tansy came into the hall.

'I went over to see Pa.' Tansy took off her outer garments.

'He reckoned that you had, miss.' The housekeeper shut the front door.

'Did he leave a message?'

'He said not to worry about going to the inquest with Mrs Simpson as he's offered to escort her himself and not to fret if you don't hear from him for a couple of days. He's following up a story.'

'Thank you, Mrs Timothy.'

Tansy felt as if she'd been kicked. So Frank imagined that she would fret if she didn't see him for a few days, did he? Frank had a lot to learn about her habits of emotional independence!

'I'll have a cup of coffee if you please,' she said aloud.

'Right away, miss!' Mrs Timothy bustled off.

Tansy, going to the front window, looped back the lace curtains and looked out into the dying afternoon. The street-lamps were not yet lit and the pavements were gloomy, spiked with dark shadows.

'Is anything wrong, miss?' Mrs Timothy, coming in with coffee, asked the question in as shocked a tone as if Tansy had hung a red lantern in the window.

'Every house in this neighbourhood has lace curtains at the front windows!' she said crossly.

'To stop folk from looking in and seeing what's going on, what we're up to,' Mrs Timothy said, twitching them into place as Tansy moved away.

'In this house nothing ever goes on and nobody,' said Tansy, 'ever gets up to anything!'

'Your pa's all right?' Her housekeeper prepared to sympathize.

'Pa is fine,' Tansy said. 'Sorry, Mrs Timothy but I am in an ill temper today.'

'Maybe it's yesterday's funeral. Makes some people a bit down contemplating their own end,' Mrs Timothy said.

'I need some exercise, that's all! I've not yet reached the stage of contemplating my own end!' Tansy said crisply. 'I spend too much time riding round in cabs! I think I shall go for a walk! I'll have some dinner when I come in. Where's Tilde?'

'Writing a poem.' Mrs Timothy sniffed. 'A waste of time if you were to ask me, but quite honestly she does her work nicely and don't answer me back so I reckon she isn't doing much harm when she sets down and makes up rhymes.'

Tansy drank her coffee, put on hat and jacket again and went out.

She and Geoffrey had taken long walks, she recalled, exploring every corner of London, visiting every out of the way museum, while he had talked happily about the various digs he had been on, the thrill of finding an Etruscan vase buried under layers of shale and dirt!

What I need, Tansy thought, striding between the unlit lamps, is some gainful occupation! I know it was John Simpson I saw and that means someone else is lying in his grave!

The lamplighter had arrived, moving along the road, pausing at each bracket to kindle the gas-flame. Much of London was illumined by electricity these days but she preferred the gentler radiance of the gas-lamps.

'Miss Clark?'

A voice intruded on her musings. Tansy looked round for the owner of the voice just as a hand tugged at the peplum of her jacket.

'Miss Tansy Clark?'

She looked down at the small messenger-boy in his pill-box hat and blue tunic.

'Yes?'

'Message for you, miss!' He thrust a letter into her hand, turned and scampered off.

'Wait a minute!' Tansy started after him but he had already turned the corner.

'Anything wrong, miss?'

The lamplighter, holding his pole aloft with dignity, made the enquiry as he crossed the street towards her.

'Nothing, thank you. Good evening.'

Aware that when the lamplighter had completed his task she would be solitary in the street she retraced her steps to her own house.

'Good evening, Miss Tansy!' Tilde opened the door. 'Mrs Timothy has started dinner and I'm going to help her. Writing poetry makes one exceedingly hungry.'

'I can imagine,' Tansy said, going into her sitting-room. She closed the door, gently but firmly, lest Tilde should take it into her head to read her composition aloud. She slit open the sealed envelope. The square piece of paper within bore a short message.

Dear Madam,
I understand you are taking an interest in the sad demise of Mr John Simpson. If you could meet me either this evening or tomorrow evening at the White Bull restaurant in Crescent Street, I have private information to impart to you. Please bring this with you as a means of identification.

Yours Faithfully,
Philip Johnson

Biting her lip, Tansy slowly read the note again.

TEN

No definite hour had been specified in the note. Tansy, having eaten a hasty meal, refusing the dessert on the grounds she had a sudden engagement, changed into a neat brown outfit which would blend into any surroundings and, having told Mrs Timothy and Tilde not to wait up, set out for the cab-stand.

'Crescent Street, miss?' The driver peered at her doubtfully when she gave her destination. 'If you please.'

'It's a bit rough, that district, miss.'

'To the White Bull restaurant if you please,' Tansy added firmly.

The cabby gave a shrug and cast his eyes up to heaven as if to demand what respectable ladies were coming to. Tansy, in the cab, gave him a sweet smile as he closed the door.

Now she peered expectantly through the cab windows as it bowled through the lamplit streets. The streets were becoming more winding and narrow, and the spaces between the gas-lamps wider. They had driven eastward and were beyond Whitechapel, its cheerful evening bustle superseded by darker, badly paved thoroughfares. She glimpsed the odd figure moving along or standing in an alley, felt instinctively the pale stench of poverty.

Perhaps it had been a mistake to come here alone? She could have gone to her father's house and requested that Finn accompany her. That worthy knew every crack and crevice of the East End, knew every cracksmith, pimp and dosser, and had a formidable left hook though in his previous career it had been used most frequently against the forces of law and order.

'We're here, miss!'

The cab swayed to a stop and the driver climbed down to open the door.

Tansy stepped down, paid the fare, adding a tip despite her resolve not to because he really didn't deserve one for making it clear that he regarded females as weak and feeble creatures, and looked about her with a tingle of apprehension.

The White Bull restaurant was smaller than she had envisaged, tucked between two other buildings with a narrow alley which led to what looked like a yard, and a swinging door through which customers were coming and going. A couple of girls, skirts hitched to their knees to show the bedraggled flounces of their petticoats, leaned against the wall, one of them complaining loudly in terms that would have horrified Mrs Timothy that her client had short-changed her, the other nodding a head adorned with a feathered hat and repeating:

'You done right, Glory! You done right!'

'Would you,' said the cabby in an irritatingly fatherly tone 'like me to wait for you, miss?'

'I am due to meet someone here,' Tansy confessed, 'but I am not certain at what hour – no, it is best if you don't wait. I shall be perfectly all right.'

'Very good, miss.'

He gave her, she thought, an odd look as he moved away, as if she wasn't the lady he had taken her to be.

If Pa knew she were here he might be tempted to jump to the same conclusion, she thought with an inward smile.

She went up to the door and looked through as its two halves swung back and forth.

'Restaurant' was a misnomer. The interior more resembled a tavern, though there were small tables with checked cloths on them and cutlery set neatly. At the far end a barmaid was dispensing drinks and jokes in equal measure to the customers crowding round and the air was hazy with smoke.

It would be more prudent to slip in through a side door, she decided, turning on impulse and making her way down the side of the building to where the narrow alley ended in an archway leading into a large yard where several horses were tethered. One of the horses whinnied, no doubt startled by her approach, and in that fleeting second she glimpsed a figure slip from behind a cart and melt into the darkness. It might have nothing to do with the note that had brought her here but Tansy, who was still apt on occasion to act on impulse instead of with what Laurence called 'reasoned caution', promptly followed.

To her right, where the dark shape had fled, a narrow gate stood partly ajar giving egress from the yard into a winding street with warehouses looming along both sides.

As a child she had played at following suspects with her father. Now the old training reasserted itself and she stood very still, her eyes gradually becoming accustomed to the dark.

A sleek furry shape suddenly streaked across from one building to the other, uttering the long-drawn howl of a hunting feline. Tansy drew in her breath with a sharp gasp and in that moment saw the black shadow of a man thrown across the cobbles by the guttering light of a feeble lamp over a doorway.

He must have come from one of the warehouses, she supposed, the deeper blackness there indicating the presence of an open door. Someone was making a fool of her with a game of hoodman blind; she took a pace forward just as with a swooshing sound a large jagged stone missed her by inches and fell at her feet.

The shock was so great that she was frozen for a moment, turned to ice by the realization that this was very far from being a game!

Behind her footsteps pounded across the street and a voice called,

'What in the world is happening? Are you hurt?'

'No, I – it fell short,' Tansy gasped, half turning.

'Are you certain?' The voice was familiar but she was unable to place it.

'Henry Oakley, Miss Clark.' He had doffed his hat. 'We met the other evening. You were with Frank Cartwright.'

'What are you doing here?' she asked bewildered.

'I received a note requesting a meeting at the White Bull,' Oakley said. 'Are you sure you're not hurt?'

'The stone fell short,' Tansy said shiveringly. He bent and picked it up, weighing it in his hand. 'That's a vicious piece of rock,' he said slowly. 'Had it hit you . . .'

Footsteps were running towards them across the yard as he drew her back through the gateway.

'You all right, miss?' a voice called.

'My cab driver! He did offer to wait!' She felt a surge of relief as she raised her own voice to call, 'I'm a trifle shaken, nothing more! You need not have waited.'

'Rough place for a respectable lady,' the cab driver said in a disapproving tone. 'I saw this cove come after you and—'

'An acquaintance of mine.' Tansy was swiftly regaining her composure. 'I was following someone else who heaved a large stone at me and most fortunately missed. He is gone now and I came to no harm.'

'If you're sure you're all right, miss?'

Cheated of some heroic act with which he might have regaled his friends, the driver touched his forelock and turned reluctantly towards the alley.

'May I suggest you have a brandy, Miss Clark, or a glass of wine?' Henry Oakley offered his arm. 'Something here needs to be investigated.'

'Thank you, sir. A glass of wine if you please.'

Taking his arm as he guided her across the yard and down the alley to the main entrance of the White Bull she controlled her trembling.

Not until she was seated in a discreetly inconspicuous corner with a glass of wine before her did the cold sick feeling begin to decrease. It was succeeded by the sense of having found the best way to make a complete fool of herself!

'You were coming to meet someone, Mr Oakley?' she said.

'I received a note this afternoon while I was at my office. I was asked to bring it with me either tonight or tomorrow. Here it is.'

He passed her the envelope and she took out the folded piece of paper.

'The message is the same as the one that I received,' she said, scanning it rapidly.

'From a Philip Johnson?'

'Yes, from someone called Philip Johnson.'

'Who then is Philip Johnson?' he enquired.

'I've no idea. I know nobody of that name.'

'And yet you came alone? That was brave of you, Miss Clark.'

'It was exceedingly stupid!' she said impatiently. 'I ought to have come with an escort. My problem is that I am always too eager to prove my independence!'

'That can be a charming trait in an intelligent woman,' he said.

'If you hadn't also received a message – if that stone had hit me . . .' She bit her lip, staring into her wine.

'Perhaps you disturbed a robber?' he suggested.

'I don't think so.' She shook her head. 'I thought it might be wiser to look around first instead of walking straight in. I went down the side of the building hoping to slip in unobtrusively by a side door. There was someone in the yard and he ran. I saw him run.'

'Did you recognize him?'

'It was too dark,' she said regretfully. 'I saw only the figure and I suspect that he had just tethered his horse when he saw me and ran away.'

'I hadn't realized that you were so formidable, Miss Clark,' he said with a slight smile.

'Then perhaps he was stealing a horse? Or he ran hoping that I might be lured into following him.'

'Then he must know you by sight at least!'

'Or he was just hoping to rob someone or go through the saddlebags? No, I cannot believe that!' Tansy sipped her wine. 'When I reached the yard I stood still for a moment. Then I glimpsed him – just a dark figure moving – and then I did follow him towards that gateway, but cautiously! I wasn't chasing after him. I'm not quite so foolish as that! He threw the stone at me when he could have simply melted into the darkness.'

'At the very least that stone might have hurt you greatly,' Oakley said frowningly. 'Miss Clark, are you sure that you don't know a Philip Johnson?'

'I'm absolutely sure,' Tansy said. 'Mr Oakley, this isn't the first time someone has flung a jagged stone at me. The first time it occurred it could have been an accident but twice . . . !'

'What happened?' he asked.

She related the incident in the park.

'One cannot imagine that two different people would've tried to injure you in the same manner – if the two incidents were connected.'

'I'm sure they were. Neither stone actually hit me which means either that he has a poor aim or that he wishes only to frighten me.'

'The investigation mentioned in the note,' Oakley said. 'That refers to the sad case of the young man whose manuscript I rejected.'

'John Simpson, yes.'

'A friend of his might have wished to disturb me by sending such a note but – investigation?' He raised his dark brows.

'There's some reason to believe that John Simpson might have been murdered,' Tansy said.

'I thought he was drowned!'

'He was but he was tied by his left wrist to the water wheel and it transpires that he was left-handed. You see?'

'Of course. A left-handed man would have tied his right wrist to the wheel.'

'What I cannot understand,' Tansy mused, 'is why he went to such elaborate means to kill himself – if he did indeed kill himself, or why anyone else should stage such a macabre charade.'

'A blow to the face to render him unconscious? Then if he was murdered, which I personally find hard to accept, he was borne to the water wheel and fastened there.'

'When it would've been equally efficient simply to push him into the river?'

'Where he might have been carried out to sea or washed up months later.'

'It was his wife who found him,' Tansy said soberly.

'At least she has the certainty of grief instead of the uncertainty of not knowing what had happened to him.'

'Would a murderer care about that?' Tansy queried.

'No, but John Simpson himself might have considered it,' Oakley said slowly. 'Only think of his state of mind, Miss Clark! His book rejected – he has a young wife dependent on him and no steady income—'

'Verity Simpson did tell me that he was subject to depression,' Tansy put in.

'He wanders around town, decides to make an end of it all, but he wants to spare his wife the long waiting so he wades out into the river, ties himself to the wheel and is drowned and crushed – knowing that before long his body will be discovered.'

'But he tied himself by the wrong hand,' Tansy objected.

'Perhaps he was ambidextrous. Very few people are entirely left- or right-handed.'

'My father would agree with you,' she allowed. 'He's a retired police officer who still takes a keen interest in certain criminal cases.'

'And you interest yourself in what delights your father? That is a most admirable trait, Miss Clark.'

'As you did,' Tansy said. 'Your publishing house was begun by your father and you carried it on.'

'Hoping to discover a masterpiece!' He grimaced, caught her eye and gave a rueful smile. 'So far it hasn't happened but this is the first time a rejected author has gone away and killed himself!'

'Did you ever meet John Simpson personally?' she asked.

'No, he left his manuscript with my secretary. I read it over – skipped it rather, I'm ashamed to say. It was completely unsuitable for our list – for anyone's list I would've thought – but that doesn't lessen my own feelings of regret. Perhaps if I had interviewed him – suggested that he might try his hand at a different theme – I feel very badly about that.'

'But, as you say, rejected authors don't often kill themselves. He may have had other troubles, other enemies.'

'I imagine the verdict at the inquest will be suicide. Are you going to the wretched affair?'

'I doubt if I'll be called,' Tansy said. 'I know nothing first hand. However I feel that I ought to accompany Mrs Simpson. I went with her to the funeral.'

'I didn't attend,' Oakley said. 'I felt it more tactful to stay away. How would the poor lady have felt, knowing that my rejection of his book probably was partly to blame for his death?'

'But you will testify at the inquest?'

'I've agreed to do so though I fear that after my evidence the stock of publishers will fall even lower than it is already!' He gave a rueful smile as he finished his wine.

Around them the 'restaurant' was still crowded and noisy. The women coming in were by now so tipsy that several of them were being ejected, one of them flinging out a hand towards the table where Tansy and her escort sat, to splutter:

'Why ain't you chucking 'er aht then?'

'The hour grows late,' Oakley said. 'May I take you home?'

'Yes. Thank you, yes.' Tansy rose, avoiding the glances slanted in her direction.

'It was fortunate that I decided to come,' Oakley said as he ushered her through the door. 'This is definitely not the place for a lady!'

'I came on impulse,' Tansy admitted.

'A charming trait but sometimes impractical. These notes will have to be given to the police since they both refer to John Simpson. I'll take them round first thing in the morning,' he said. 'They may be a rather unpleasant practical joke but they ought to be reported.'

'My father isn't going to be terribly pleased to learn that I rushed off by myself without even telling anyone where I was going,' Tansy said.

'If I requested discretion where you were concerned your father isn't likely to hear of it. The notes are hardly likely to form any part of the evidence at the inquest.'

'That would be very kind of you, Mr Oakley.' Tansy stepped back as a cab slowed and stopped at the corner of the street.

'Where do you live?'

'Chelsea.' She gave the address to the cabby.

'Drop me off at my office first,' Oakley instructed. 'Fleet Street.'

'You must work very hard,' Tansy said, settling herself in the cab.

'I don't usually work at night, Miss Clark, but it just occurred to me that some author who has also had his work rejected, even a disgruntled reader, who dislikes something that I published, might be seeking to cause mischief. Whoever it is must know of us both. Leave me to deal with it as far as possible. At least no harm has arisen from this adventure!'

'You arrived in the nick of time and I haven't thanked you properly yet,' Tansy said warmly.

'I'm only glad that I was there in time to avert what might have been a most unhappy experience. And I shall find out what lies behind this, never fear!'

It was a relief to have someone who was prepared to deal with the situation without involving her more than was necessary.

'This is where I alight!' He rapped sharply on the trapdoor. 'Miss Clark, I hope you won't feel that I'm seeking to take advantage of the situation but having now met you twice I feel it wouldn't be too improper to invite you to have dinner with me – or lunch. Whichever you prefer. It may turn out that we both have a mutual acquaintance named Philip Johnson!'

'After the inquest – when you've spoken to the police – we shall see,' Tansy said. 'It would be very pleasant.'

'With which hope I shall bid you good-night, Miss Clark!'

He stepped down on to the pavement and doffed his hat as the cab was driven away.

Tansy felt an unaccustomed glow of satisfaction. Her fright at the near-injury she had suffered was mitigated by the feeling that for the first time in many years an attractive and successful man wished to further his acquaintance with her.

Another thought drifted into her head as they bowled towards Chelsea. By accepting Henry Oakley's invitation she would be showing Frank Cartwright that she wasn't without male admirers!

ELEVEN

Tansy, having finished her breakfast and ignored Tilde's hopefully questioning looks about the previous evening, put on her straw hat and walked round to The Larches. The windows of the house were still shrouded but Verity opened the door fairly promptly, her face still pale but her eyes brighter than before. She was wearing a black dress with soft lace ruffles at neck and sleeves and her fair ringlets were bunched at the back of her neck with black ribbon.

'Miss Clark – Tansy! How good of you to come,' she said, her features breaking into a smile. 'Do please come in.'

'You look better,' Tansy said as she was ushered into the hall.

'I have the most astounding news,' Verity said. 'Please come into the sitting-room. I lit a fire here and have just brewed some coffee. You will have some?'

'Thank you.' Tansy obediently seated herself, glancing at the table, but the wedding photograph was no longer in sight.

'Black or white?' Verity was fussing with cups.

'Black please, and only half a cup. I breakfasted late. Have the police been with any further information?'

'The police? No. No, they've not contacted me.'

'I merely called to ask how you are and whether or not you required my company at the inquest, or is Mr Cartwright . . . ?'

'Such a charming gentleman, isn't he? He's not what I always thought a newspaper reporter would be like at all. So helpful and so sympathetic!' Verity said. 'You are indeed fortunate to have such a friend. I hope you don't think it improper of me to have lunch with him so soon after poor John died? He would not have wanted me to cry my life away.'

'I imagine not,' Tansy said. 'Will you be wanting my maid to come and help you in the house?'

'That's my news!' Verity handed her the coffee and sat down, clasping her hands tightly together. 'I am leaving The Larches. Indeed I have already begun to pack!'

'Leaving? But I thought the rent was paid ahead – not that it's any of my business.'

Tansy swallowed a mouthful of the weak coffee and put cup and saucer on the table.

'My great-aunt – Caroline – I think I mentioned her—'

'Has asked you to make your home with her? Then I'm pleased for your sake that the family quarrel is mended.'

'I had word yesterday,' Verity said breathlessly, 'that Aunt Caroline has died. A letter from her solicitor informing me that she had died the day before my dear John was buried.'

'How did she die?' Tansy asked.

'She had been ill for many years.' Verity looked somewhat startled at the question. 'Her heart was weak. I have the letter here, Tansy. I have been reading it over and over trying to believe it. It's quite incredible, really it is!'

She took a letter out of her pocket and handed it over.

'Your great-aunt died on Monday morning?' Tansy said, scanning the copperplate writing with the engraved heading.

'In the early hours of the morning,' Verity nodded. 'The doctor was with her and Mr Parrish, her solicitor, was also called in. I wish I had known how very sick she truly was. I would have gone to see her, really I would!'

'And you are her sole heir?' Tansy said, looking at the letter again.

'It seems that I am. Somehow that pricks my conscience even more. She has left me her own little house where she lived all her life.'

'It's an ill wind . . .' Tansy said helplessly.

'I have determined to leave London as soon as possible,' Verity told her. 'Yes. Yes, I see! You think me heartless to seize my legacy.'

'I think nothing of the kind,' Tansy said. 'Naturally you want to leave a place where you have known great unhappiness.'

'And how I shall wish that dear John were with me!' Verity said, her eyes filling up. 'To start afresh will be very hard. Do you know the Midlands?'

Tansy shook her head.

'She is to be buried on Saturday,' Verity was continuing. 'I feel that I ought to be there. I wish that I had gone to see her sooner. It's a sad affair, is it not, that I should have missed the chance of a reconciliation with my only relative? My only consolation is that the quarrel was long-standing and not of my making. I have written to Mr Parrish signyfying my intentions.' Verity paused, stifling a sob as she took the letter back. 'If only John had known then perhaps he would never have . . .' She shook her head slowly.

'If you need any help with your packing . . .' Tansy murmured. Her conscience had begun to prick her. She had actually been feeling jealous of the pretty little widow, she admitted to herself. Like a silly dog in the manger she had held Frank at arm's length while resenting his interest in Verity.

'We have very few possessions of our own,' Verity said. 'I've resolved to give John's clothes to charity. He would have approved of that. My own bits and pieces will fit into a small trunk. For the rest – I must write to the landlord and ask for a refund on the rent. I hope he won't be difficult about it. John always dealt with such matters. I will tell Mr Cartwright tomorrow – the last week has flown by like some bad dream.'

Tansy, in whose experience bad dreams seemed to last for ever, murmured something indeterminate.

'It's strange,' Verity was continuing, 'how when one prepares to leave a place one suddenly finds friends. You have been very kind and so has Mr Cartwright.'

'You've not seen him?' For the life of her she couldn't stop herself from asking.

'Not since the day of the funeral. He took me for a lovely long luncheon and escorted me home. He had other business to transact.'

'Then I will see you at the inquest.' Tansy rose.

'I've been thinking . . .' Verity hesitated as her guest rose. 'I wonder if it could have been an accident. John was frequently depressed. But he would never have left me to struggle on alone. He had no enemy in the world, you know. He had no quarrel with any living soul and since he had nothing to leave his death benefited nobody.'

'No indeed,' Tansy said. Her tone was somewhat abstracted

and she had stiffened slightly.

'Until tomorrow, then.' Verity fluttered to the front door like a small black moth.

Tansy walked slowly down the short path and turned in the direction of her own house. For an instant when she reached her own gate she stood motionless, her hand upon the fence post. Her eyes saw not the fragrantly scented little garden but the somewhat bleak sitting-room she had just left.

Verity had been alone. Why then had two of the coffee cups been used? One half-drunk with the spoon still in it, as if someone had been stirring in the sugar and had risen hastily when the doorbell rang.

She went up the narrow path along the side of the house, on to the terrace through the side door there. Through the open window she could hear Tilde chattering away and Mrs Timothy answering. A bee flew over her head and buried itself in a clump of blossom.

Without pausing to think further or to work out any plan of action she went down the steps and into the garden proper.

Pa had trained her to use her eyes and her common sense. He had always warned her against jumping to conclusions. Verity might easily have put too much sugar into her cup of coffee and, rather than carry it to the kitchen and wash it, had simply poured a second measure into a second cup. And Verity was leaving town, going to live up in Derbyshire. At least she had a home to go to and that meant that her own suspicions about Frank were entirely unjustified.

Yet something still nagged at the back of her mind, formless, refusing to come into the light.

She picked a bunch of mixed blossoms from the flowering

beds confining herself to white and mauve and tied them neatly with a long stalk of grass. This would, if necessary, serve as her excuse.

'Will you be needing a vase for those, Miss Tansy?' Mrs Timothy called, coming out on to the terrace. 'I was thinking of getting Tilde to give them a bit of a wash but if you need one . . . ?'

'I'm taking these to Mrs Simpson,' Tansy called back.

'Right! We'll get on then!'

Tansy waved and stepped over the wall on to the riverbank. She walked slowly, ideas revolving in her mind. Pa had taught her something as well as common sense and alertness. He had taught her to trust her deepest instincts, and at this moment her deepest instincts warned her that the extra used coffee-cup deserved investigation.

Unless Verity had treated the postman to a cup of coffee she hadn't been alone in the house. Someone had been drinking coffee with her behind the drawn curtains of the sitting-room and had quickly absented themselves when the doorbell had sounded.

But who? Surely not Frank, who had every right to drink coffee wherever he pleased! John Simpson? But dead men didn't drink coffee with their widows. If he was dead! She recalled in vivid detail the face she had seen from the cab window. In her bones she knew there had been no mistake. Verity might have been deceived by the body with the battered face wearing her husband's clothes and ring but she had been muddled and upset. A left–handed man didn't tie his left hand to the spokes of a water wheel; a feeble swimmer didn't struggle out to the middle of a swift-flowing river and balance there while he tied secure knots; and nobody carefully removed his shoes before he drowned himself.

She had reached the back gate, still hanging on its hinges, open to the neglected back garden with its thickets of bramble and nettles. For a moment she hesitated, then walked in and took the path almost hidden between ox-eyed daisies and wickedly sharp thistles.

The back door was slightly ajar. Tansy pushed it wider and stood on the threshhold. She had unconsciously clutched her home-made bouquet more tightly, her lips silently rehearsing the words she intended to say.

I was in the garden picking some flowers when it occurred to me that you might like to have some and, as I was in the back already, I thought that . . .

She had taken a few steps into the kitchen when laughter rang out from behind the door leading into the passage.

'I see no point in trying again!'

That was Verity's voice, no longer gentle and subdued but amused and light. Her laughter trilled upon the air.

A heavier tread sounded on the floor. Tansy cast a frantic look at the door and saw the handle slowly begin to turn. For a second she was rooted to the spot and then she was crouching under the long table, hoping that the checked tablecloth concealed both herself and her flowers. The sweat had broken out on her forehead and she felt it trickle towards her eyes.

Under the checked tablecloth someone had laid another of dark chenille, its fringes dipping to the floor, blocking out the light. Tansy consoled herself with the thought that not being able to see also meant that she was herself was out of sight and she held her breath as the kitchen door creaked open. The footsteps sounded a short way into the kitchen and stopped abruptly. She heard the faint rattle of what sounded like a dish or a saucer being removed from among other crockery and then the kitchen door closed and the heavier footsteps died away down the passage.

Nobody had spoken so the identity of whoever had entered the room remained a mystery, and whoever had come in had obviously been aware of no other presence there. Nevertheless to be on the safe side she set herself to remain where she was for a few more minutes in case the other should come in again.

Her eyes were gradually becoming accustomed to the gloom. She could discern the glint of metal – a brass handle of some kind. Tansy felt cramp shoot up her calf and gingerly tried to straighten her leg, her knee coming into contact with something hard and sharp.

A dull thud from the front of the house signalled the closing of the front door. The visitor, whoever he had been, had departed. She waited a few moments more, listening for the sound of lighter footsteps in the passage but the house was silent.

Tansy crawled out from beneath the double cloths, torn between irritation at the foolish figure she had risked cutting had she been discovered and a most intense curiosity.

Verity had mentioned a small trunk into which she could pack her bits and pieces. She knelt down and lifted the cloths up, seeing the long cabin trunk with its brass fittings. That was what she'd banged her knee on, and by no stretch of the imagination could it be termed small. Stooping, she tugged at the broad leather strap that was buckled round the middle of the trunk and inched out the heavy piece of luggage, glad that the uncarpeted floor made the task slightly easier, but she was panting a little and her wrists were aching by the time she had it free of the concealing tablecloths.

Tansy sat back on her heels and wrestled with the strap. It was of broad, new leather and resisted her efforts for several minutes before she had loosened it sufficiently to pull the two ends free.

Was it locked or not? She snapped up the clasps and heaved a sigh of relief. To poke about in someone else's property was bad enough but to force a lock was definitely criminal.

She lifted the lid cautiously. Even before she looked down she tensed against the discovery of what she instinctively knew she would find.

John Simpson, the young man in the wedding photograph, the man she had glimpsed briefly from the cab window, lay there, his hands folded, his eyes closed. There was absolutely no doubt that he was very dead. She could smell the faint, sweetish smell of encroaching decay and see how the features of the dead man had set into waxy whiteness with all life drained out.

Whatever had happened to him he had not drowned nor, judging from his unmarked wrists, been tied to a water wheel.

TWELVE

Automatically she lowered the lid of the trunk and clicked it shut, each click sounding like a pistol shot in her ears. Then she buckled the broad leather strap, her fingers trembling despite her resolve to remain calm. It remained only to slide the whole back under the table and let the tablecloths fall into place, the long fringes of the chenille almost touching the floor.

There was a sound in the passage beyond the door, something between a cough and a sneeze. Tansy's nerves jangled as she rose, edged to the back door and slipped through, drawing it close behind her. A quick glance upwards showed an upper row of close-curtained windows and an instant later she was running through the neglected garden, through the gateway and thence along the riverbank to the safety of her own domain.

In her sitting-room she poured herself a small brandy and gulped it down.

'Did you have a nice walk, Miss T – is anything wrong?' Tilde came in and stopped dead to gape at her mistress.

'I slipped on a patch of mud,' Tansy invented rapidly. 'I'm not hurt in the least but my skirt and shoes are in sad case!'

'If you change them I'll see to them right away,' Tilde said, giving Tansy a comically maternal look. 'Shock can do very serious things to the constitution of an older person.'

'Then I shall take my ageing bones upstairs and change my garments,' Tansy said with a grin. 'I shall be lunching with my father.'

Upstairs she stripped off the dusty dress and grass-stained shoes and washed her hands and face. By the time she had combed and coiled her hair and donned a dark-blue skirt and jacket with a lacy white blouse she had regained her self-possession.

Nevertheless Tilde must have volunteered some distorted tale since she was confronted by Mrs Timothy as she came downstairs.

'Is everything all right, Miss Tansy? You didn't suffer any serious hurt?' she enquired anxiously.

'I am perfectly all right,' Tansy said firmly. 'I'm going to my father's for luncheon.'

'Will you be back for dinner?' Mrs Timothy wanted to know.

'I'm really not sure. Why?'

'It was only that Tilde did mention you'd told her it might be a nice outing for us to visit the music hall. I thought if we weren't required this evening . . . ?'

'By all means!' Tansy said briskly. 'Leave something cold on a tray for me in the larder and go and enjoy yourselves.'

'If you're quite certain, miss? I must say you don't look your usual self. A fall can cause delayed shock which can affect the nervous system you know. I sometimes wonder if my bad back wasn't caused by me getting down off a stepladder too hastily.'

'You enjoy your evening out,' Tansy said, avoiding further information about her housekeeper's bad back. 'I shall take my keys. Oh, this will cover cab fares and tickets and a bite of supper for you both.'

'Thank you kindly, miss! Please give your pa my very best!' Mrs Timothy sailed back into her kitchen kingdom.

Tansy was fortunate enough to see a cab depositing a neighbour several doors further down the street, hailed it as it turned and within half an hour was mounting the steps outside her father's house.

'I was just preparing lunch, Miss Tansy!' Finn said, opening the front door and looking as pleased as his lugubrious features would permit.

'For once,' said Tansy, drawing off hat and gloves, 'Pa will have to put up with my cooking! I want you to go to the police station.'

'What's happened?' Finn asked.

'Tell the inspector that if he sends round a couple of his officers to The Larches in Chelsea he will find a dead body in a trunk under the kitchen table!'

'Good Lord!' Finn stared at her. 'Are you sure, miss?'

'Of course I'm sure! I can recognize a dead body when I find one!' Tansy said indignantly. 'Hurry now! I shall finish making the lunch and then I shall tell Pa all over it.'

'Right, miss! On me way!'

Finn seized his hat and coat and went out.

Luncheon was going to be fillets of plaice with vegetables and one of Finn's sauces. Tansy took over, finding that the ordinary tasks of stirring the sauce to the requisite smoothness and arranging the vegetables in their tureen calmed her more than anything else could have done.

When she carried the lunch upstairs Laurence swivelled round in his chair and stared at her with lifted brows.

'I thought I heard voices,' he commented. 'Has Finn eloped

with the admirable Mrs Timothy, then?'

'Finn has gone to the police station to report the finding of a body and I finished the luncheon,' Tansy said.

'Who found the body? – No, don't tell me. You did!'

'In a trunk under the kitchen table in The Larches.'

'What were you doing under the kitchen table, may I ask?'

'Hiding!' Tansy said impatiently.

'Why?' He tasted the sauce and nodded approval.

Tansy briefly related the circumstances to him. 'I know it was unpardonable curiosity to open the trunk but I did and – Pa, the body was that of John Simpson!'

'Someone disturbed his grave?'

'Pa, he's never been in a grave. The man in the trunk was the same man I saw in the wedding photograph and the same man I saw from the cab window!'

'After death the features can lose individuality—'

'His hadn't, and it was John Simpson. I sent Finn to tell the police at once which is why I finished the luncheon.'

'And very tastily considering your state of mind. Tansy, I am quite ready to believe that you found a body in a trunk but can you be certain that it was John Simpson?'

'Positive – and he hadn't drowned! There were no abrasions on his wrists either. It was John Simpson and that means someone else was drowned, and buried in his name.'

'And that suggests murder to me – to you also, I think?'

'Yes, Pa.' Tansy pushed her plate aside and spoke earnestly. 'The other man could've been stunned by a blow to the back of the head – of course I couldn't see that body but that's an educated guess. Then he was dressed in John Simpson's clothes and the engraved wedding ring put on his finger. But the shoes were too small so couldn't be used and his own shoes were removed lest they be the means of identifying him. Then he was held under the water and tied to the wheel. The spokes as they turned would damage his face and make identification difficult.'

'So someone wanted people to believe that John Simpson was dead,' Laurence said thoughtfully. 'I wonder why.'

'I'm sure I'm right, Pa!' Tansy insisted.

'And now, if you're correct, John Simpson is dead, anyway.'

'So why kill someone else in the first place?'

'Wheels within wheels. I think we shall finish our lunch and reserve further discussion until Finn returns.'

'He probably insisted on going with the police to The Larches,' Tansy said, pouring coffee.

'Without a warrant?'

'Surely . . .' Tansy bit her lip.

'A good reason must be given before a search warrant is issued. You know that, Tansy!'

'I learnt it at my father's knee,' Tansy said wryly.

'That sounds like Finn!' Laurence revolved his chair as Finn tapped on the door and came in.

'I'd've got the lunch finished before I left, sir,' he said reproachfully, 'but Miss Tansy was that set on getting me out of the 'ouse!'

'And the meal turned out very nicely,' Tansy said. 'Tell us what happened!'

'I went straight to the coppers,' Finn said, 'and as it 'appens I was in luck. The duty sergeant is by way of being an admirer of yours, sir! Anyrate he goes in to speak to 'is super and off we go to The Larches! Mrs Verity Simpson was there. A very nice-spoken young lady if I might say so! Pretty too!'

'Finn, what happened then?' Tansy urged.

'Well, we put it to the young lady as there was a dead body in a trunk under 'er kitchen table. She went all of a tremble at that and I can't say as I was surprised. Not a nice thing for a young lady to 'ear! Anyway she invited us in, which, strictly speaking, I don't think she 'ad to do according to law as we'd no search warrant and I wasn't even official but she never made no song and dance about it. Kept telling us to find it and get it out of the place!'

'And did you find it?' Tansy asked.

'No, Miss Tansy,' Finn said sadly. 'No, we didn't. There was a small trunk packed with bits and pieces but no big trunk anywhere.'

'Where did you look?' Tansy demanded.

'After we looked under the kitchen table and it weren't there she begged us to look all over the 'ouse. Said she couldn't bear to think that it might be somewhere else, just waiting to pop out, so to speak!'

'Dead bodies in trunks don't just pop out!' Tansy said.

'She didn't put it in them precise terms,' Finn admitted, 'but the notion of it sent her all in a quiver! Anyway we went all over the 'ouse and the garden and not a trace of trunk or part of a body did we find!'

'Was she alone in the house?' Laurence asked.

'No sign of anyone else, and I kept my eyes peeled. Anyway there wasn't no point in looking anywhere else so the super apologized and thanked her for her time and we came away.'

'What about Mrs Simpson?' Tansy wanted to know.

'She said she's going to the Midlands tomorrow after the inquest,' Finn said. 'An auntie's died – first her 'usband and now her auntie! Bad luck don't come singly, that's certain!'

'Without a trunk, let alone a body, there's no evidence to present to the court,' Laurence said, drumming his fingers on the arm of his chair.

'I found the trunk; I opened the trunk; the body was inside,' Tansy said tersely.

'Perhaps Frank will have some news for us when we see him,' her father said.

'Frank Cartwright is off chasing a story somewhere or other,' Tansy said sourly. 'He has promised to escort Verity Simpson to the inquest tomorrow or so she told me. The whole affair will be a complete farce in my opinion! The truth is quite different from what the coroner will be told and nothing can be done now because we have no proof!'

'Nevertheless, my girl, you will not go letting yourself into other people's houses again without permission,' Laurence warned.

'You didn't . . .?' Tansy looked at Finn.

'No, miss, 'course not! Mrs Simpson asked who'd given us the tale but the super said it were confidential information!'

'You did your best, Finn,' Tansy said.

'I did what I could, miss. Sorry the results ain't more satisfying,' Finn said.

'And you missed your lunch.'

'I pays no account to that,' Finn assured her. 'Anyways it made a nice change for me – riding in a cab with two bobbies and me on the right side of the law!'

'You may end up going in for detection yourself,' Tansy said.

Finn snorted slightly. 'I aint quite that law-abiding yet, miss!' he said.

'Go down and get yourself something to eat,' Laurence ordered.

'I've a nice bit of cold eel pie waiting,' Finn said, sweeping the used dishes on to the tray and going out.

'That was a waste of time!' Tansy said, cramming on her hat in frustration. 'I ought to have reported the matter myself at once instead of which I rushed home, washed, changed my skirts – even had a tot of brandy to steady my nerves. Verity Simpson had ample time to get rid of that trunk!'

'If she knew it was there,' Laurence remarked.

'But surely . . . ?'

'Is she the sort of woman who sweeps under the kitchen table every day?'

'I doubt if she does it once a week,' Tansy told him. 'But I heard a man's footsteps in the passage – quite heavy footsteps – and she was talking to someone. Pa, who on earth can the man in the grave marked for John Simpson be?'

'I've not read any items about anyone missing in the newspapers,' he said. 'Of course he may not have been reported missing yet. Many men work away from home or live alone without family or close friends. I shall keep my eyes open.'

'And I must get off home. Mrs Timothy and Tilde have scarcely laid eyes on me in recent days.'

'My dear, you will take care?' Laurence looked at her.

'I always do, Pa!' she answered lightly.

'I hope so.'

It would only worry him to learn of the two incidents when stones had been flung at her, she decided, blowing him a kiss as she went out and ran down the stairs.

'Don't get up, Finn! Enjoy your eel pie!' she said brightly as she went through the front door.

'You will take care, Miss Tansy?' He had followed her to the steps. 'You won't go poking in other people's kitchens?'

'I'll take care!' She lifted her hand in a gesture of acceptance and walked briskly to the cab-stand.

'Where to, miss?' The cabby had climbed down and opened the cab door.

Tansy hesitated. She had every intention of going home but at the back of her mind something stirred like a negative held in developing fluid, the outlines gradually becoming more distinct.

'Regent Street,' she heard herself say. 'To Regent Street if you please.'

Not everybody who went missing was reported missing immediately. Some were never reported at all! The flotsam and jetsam fell through the cracks of civilization and the world went on without noticing that it was a little emptier.

She alighted in the street, amused as always by the people who seemed to have nothing better to do than gaze into shop windows at the goods in them, or stroll up and down nodding to acquaintances. Half the world worked too hard and the other half avoided work whenever possible!

The bell over the recessed door of Curry's Photographic Studio tinkled as she stepped in. Behind the long counter Mr Wilks was pasting some photographs into an album, but he beamed as he looked up.

'Miss Clark! How very pleasant to see you again! I am just preparing an album for a lady client who wished to keep a record of her little girl up to her seventh birthday. She brings her in every year and each study of the child has been most charming!'

'Mr Wilks, is Mr Curry back yet?' Tansy cut abruptly into his flow of chatter.

'No, Miss Clark, he isn't,' said Mr Wilks, closing the album and coming round the end of the counter. 'To tell you the truth I am rather at a loss what to do. I went round to his lodgings this morning, something I would never normally dream of doing. His landlady told me she has not seen him for several days. though he gave no intimation of his leaving.'

'Did you go inside his rooms?'

'Oh no, miss! I couldn't possibly think of doing that!' Mr Wilks said, looking shocked. 'An employee ought not to intrude—'

'But when the employer is missing, surely—'

'Oh, I'm sure that Mr Curry is not missing!' Mr Wilks sounded even more shocked. 'He is merely absent! And of course his feeling able to go away for a while leaving me in charge, so to speak, is in its way rather a subtle compliment!'

'But he doesn't usually go away without leaving word of his whereabouts?'

'No, he leaves a forwarding address when he indulges himself in a few days' holiday. It really isn't like him at all! Rather worrying as a matter of fact!'

He took off his spectacles, polished them with a handkerchief and put them back on his nose.

'Is Mr Curry elderly?' Tansy enquired.

'Oh no, Miss Clark, he's quite a young man,' Mr Wilks said.

'What does he look like?'

'Oh, I can show you!' Mr Wilks cheered up at once. 'When I first came to work here, to learn the craft, I was allowed to use the camera from time to time and I photographed Mr Curry on several occasions. We had an idea of using a photograph as an advertisement but Mr Curry decided, wisely in my opinion, that to advertise in so blatantly personal a way might be considered rather vulgar.'

'Do you still have a photograph?'

'Somewhere! One moment!' He dived behind the counter again and came up with a cardboard box.

'If one exists then it will be here,' he said. 'I keep meaning to catalogue them but – ah yes, here we are! This was taken about three years ago.'

He handed over the photograph which was already beginning to fade.

'What colouring does he have?' Tansy squinted in an effort to bring the picture into focus.

'Sandy hair, Miss Clark. I was hoping for a soft-focus study but it was too ambitious for my skills at that time. I shall of course be closing the studio during the inquest tomorrow,' Mr Wilks went on. 'I only hope that Mr Curry doesn't turn up and think me remiss in my duty.'

'Mr Wilks, I wouldn't feel too badly about closing during the inquest tomorrow,' Tansy said. 'May I keep this?'

'I'm very sorry, Miss Clark, but it's not permitted to hand out photographs without Mr Curry's express consent,' he said in a fluster. 'I shall of course keep it safely if there should be a possibility of its being needed.'

'I believe that it might be,' Tansy said sombrely.

'Then I will put it in a safe place.'

He looked unhappily confused as she left the studio and when she glanced back she saw his pale countenance, gold-rimmed spectacles slightly askew, gazing after her as she turned into the main street.

The dead man in the trunk had been John Simpson and the man now lying in John Simpson's grave was Mr Curry, photographer. Of that she was certain, but proving it would be quite a different matter!

A cheerful voice from the other side of the street stopped her in her tracks.

'Good afternoon, Miss Clark! I thought it was you!'

Henry Oakley dodged through the afternoon shoppers to reach her side.

'No ill effects from your little adventure last night?' He took her hand as she paused.

'None, thanks to your quick thinking,' Tansy assured him. 'Did you take the two notes to the police? What did they say?'

'Not very much,' he said wryly. 'They appeared to regard them as some kind of practical joke. One officer suggested that as we are both unattached it might've been a roundabout way of introducing us. I fear the police are not always intelligent in their reasoning.'

'That's what Pa says!' Tansy told him.

'And you agree with him?'

'I haven't mentioned last night's episode to him. Pa grants me my independence but he does worry about me since I'm his only child.'

'And despite his enlightened views he still regards you as being in need of protection. I am inclined to agree with him, Miss Clark. However I stand firmly by my opinion that women are as courageous as men and often far more clear thinking!'

'And the police are wrong.' Tansy said hotly. 'Mr Oakley, the drowned man wasn't John Simpson. I found John Simpson's body this morning hidden in a trunk under Verity Simpson's table!'

'His widow? How on earth did that come about?'

'I went round to see her and found myself in the kitchen.' She had the grace to blush slightly as she remembered. 'There was a trunk under the kitchen table and I – well, I opened it. The police were told but when they went round to the house the trunk had vanished.'

'Miss Clark, I don't understand any of this,' Oakley said in bewilderment. 'Mrs Simpson – she was distressed by her hmsband's death?'

'Yes. Deeply distressed. She is one of those delicate, pretty young girls who cannot cope with life unless she has a husband. She was exceedingly upset when called upon to identify her husband, so upset that she could well have made a mistake.'

'I will think twice before I reject another manuscript,' Oakley said with a grimace. 'Miss Clark, I have some business to deal with at my office but may I call you a cab?'

'No. No thank you, Mr Oakley.'

'You've certainly given me a great deal to ponder.' he said drily. 'I trust we can meet again very soon?'

'Yes. Yes, that would be pleasant. Oh, my address is—'

'Chelsea – you told the cab driver the other time we met.'

'Only last night. So much has happened since.'

'Indeed it has. Good day for now, Miss Clark. I shall call upon you when I've made further enquiries myself.'

'I live at number fifteen. I never gave the house a name.'

'On which street?'

'Park Road. I shall look forward to your calling.'

And if Frank Cartwright came strolling back when his present assignment was done she was determined to present him with a neat solution to the mystery, she decided.

But without the photograph of Mr Curry it might prove impossible to identify the body that had been buried as John Simpson, and which must at some time be exhumed.

Turning she walked rapidly back to the studio and let herself in, the bell above the door tinkling as she did so.

The front part of the studio with its long counter was empty. Mr Wilks had evidently taken himself off for a cup of tea or was in the darkroom. Tansy struggled with her conscience for at least ten seconds and then walked purposefully to the back of the counter where beneath the shining top, open shelves were piled with albums and papers.

He hadn't locked the photograph away at all. It lay on top of the first pile she slid out. Tansy thrust it inside her jacket and left the premises, rushing to lose herself in the crowd as guiltily as if she had just robbed a bank.

THIRTEEN

The air of expectancy was almost tangible when Tilde opened the door.

'Mrs Timothy says that we're both off to the music hall this evening,' she bubbled. 'I'm going to wear my best dress and my hat with the cherries on it.'

'You will look charming,' Tansy said warmly.

'You're liable to forget your head let alone find your best hat!' Mrs Timothy scolded, appearing majestically at the kitchen door. 'Cold chicken cuts and a nice lemon tart all right for you, Miss Tansy? I've put them in the pantry and covered them over though I'd call the Lord Chief High Justice to witness that no fly lasts longer than two minutes in this house!'

'That will do splendidly, Mrs Timothy,' Tansy approved.

'Go upstairs and make ready, Tilde!' Mrs Timothy nodded at her underling. 'Not that she deserves to go anywhere, Miss Tansy, for she's spent most of the day dreaming through the window at every draycart that passes.'

'It wasn't a draycart!' Tilde, half-way up the stairs, paused to protest. 'I was cleaning the front windows, Miss Tansy, and a carriage went by. It went past and stopped just round the corner outside The Larches.'

'It's clever of you to be able to see round corners,' Tansy observed drily.

'Well, I did just nip down to the gate for a moment,' Tilde admitted. 'I daresay it was taking poor Mrs Simpson's things over to the railway station.'

'The poor lady'll not want to stay where there are sad memories,' Mrs Timothy agreed.

'Being a widow,' sighed Tilde, 'must be very romantic!' With which observation she resumed her ascent.

'Shall I brew you some tea or coffee before we set out?' Mrs Timothy enquired.

'Go and get yourself ready. I am quite capable of making myself a hot drink!' Tansy said, amused.

'Well, if you're sure, miss! An evening out will perk Tilde and me up no end,' Mrs Timothy said, 'and the sitting won't be bad for my back, either – not that I ever complain of it!'

'Indeed you don't, Mrs Timothy,' Tansy said solemnly.

A long, quiet evening lay ahead of her. She wasn't sorry for it since it seemed to her that she had spent a great deal of recent time dashing up promising avenues that led to blind alleys.

It was another three-quarters of an hour before Mrs Timothy and Tilde departed for their evening out, the former resplendent in her best figured black satin with a turban cap trimmed with white feathers, the latter looking bewitching in her cherry-decorated hat.

Twilight was stealing over the garden. Tansy saw them out and went into the sitting-room to light the lamps against the gathering dusk.

When you're stuck with a problem go back to the beginning and question every assumption you've ever made.

With her father's advice echoing in her head she sat down at her desk and drew a sheet of writing-paper towards her.

Picking up a pencil and staring for a moment at the blank paper she began to write.

John Simpson, small feet, left-handed, wanted to go to sea but began writing instead though not very successfully. Married to Verity, small, frail, and very pretty. They have exchanged engraved rings on their marriage and had a photograph taken at the Curry Photographic Studio. They rent house in Chelsea. John Simpson submits manuscript to Henry Oakley. Rejected. Disappears for forty-eight hours. Body found tied to water wheel in river. Tied by left wrist to spoke. Face damaged. Engraved ring on finger. No shoes on feet. Pronounced dead for two days approximately. Self saw John Simpson in street the evening after he is supposed to have died. Self receives attempted attack in park. Self receives note from a Philip Johnson asking me to meet him at the White Bull. Self goes to stable yard and sees lurking figure. Follows and has stone flung at her. Further attacks prevented by arrival of Henry Oakley. He has also received a note from a Philip Johnson. Another man in house when I visit Verity Simpson – two used coffee-cups and heavy footsteps in hall. Self finds body of John Simpson in trunk under table in kitchen of The Larches. Self returns to studio. Mr Curry still absent. Is he the man buried as John Simpson? Self returns to studio and takes photograph of Mr Curry.

She paused, chewing the end of her pencil and then wrote rapidly:

Police find no trunk or body in The Larches. Police refuse to take the two Philip Johnson notes seriously. Carriage taking Verity's things to the railway? Verity's aunt died and left her a small legacy, also a house, despite family rift. Where is the manuscript of John Simpson's rejected book?

All questions and no real answers. The evening stretched ahead even more emptily.

Tansy picked up the photograph she had taken from the studio and studied it more closely. She hadn't seen the body tied to the water wheel but Mr Curry was the right age and colouring to judge from the picture in her hand. She turned it over and noticed for the first time that an address had been scribbled on the back: *Ladymead Gardens. Regent Alley.*

Well, part of an address anyway, she conceded. And Mr Curry hadn't been into his studio for days.

She rose, put on her hat and jacket, checked the locks, put the key to the front door and the photograph into her bag and left the house. At least she could satisfy herself as to the whereabouts of Mr Curry even if Mr Wilks was too diffident to do so!

Passing The Larches she glanced towards the windows and saw that a faint light burned behind the drawn curtains. Was Verity there alone or was someone else there too?

Regent Alley was one of the narrow, badly lit streets that twisted away from the main thoroughfare with its plate-glass windows. Tansy dismissed the cab, feeling, despite her resolution, thankful that the daylight hadn't entirely faded. She entered the narrow cobbled alley and went slowly along it, past the back premises of several shops, to a short row of smaller dwelling-houses, some divided into apartments with the names of the occupants just outside the front doors.

There had been no number on the scribbled address, nor were there any signs of gardens here. She paused, looking about her uncertainly, jumping as a small boy materialized from a nearby doorway and said invitingly,

'Give us twopence, lady, and I'll show yer the way!'

'Ladymead Gardens?' Tansy instinctively tightened her grasp on her bag.

'In there! 'Tisn't a proper garden though!' the boy said.

'Are there houses there?'

'One. It's a boarding-'ouse, lady. Mrs Fletcher runs it. You don't look in need of a doss!'

'I am actually very poor,' Tansy said, fishing a threepenny bit out of her pocket. 'Thank you.'

'Thanks, lady!' The child bit the coin, rubbed it on the seat of his breeches and was gone in a flash.

Tansy pushed open the wooden door, which was already ajar, and went up a brick-paved path that ran alongside a surprisingly neat garden to the large square house at its end.

The front door was closed and there was no list of names outside it. Tansy lifted her hand and rang the bell.

'Yes?'

The woman who opened the door looked as if she had been born to run a boarding-house, her brown-silk dress with its ruffled sleeves and her upswept grey hair were in exact accord with her shrewd but good-natured face.

'Are you the lady of the house?' Tansy enquired.

'Mrs Fletcher.' The name was pronounced with dignity. 'I don't usually open the door after dusk unless one of my gentlemen has left his key, which seldom happens on account of all my gentlemen are of the highest professional standing. I'm afraid we have no vacancies at all.'

'No, I am not looking for accommodation,' Tansy said.

'And visitors of the opposite gender are not permitted after six in the evening, unless they are relatives.'

'My name is Tansy Clark. My father was Inspector —'

'Laurence Clark! He got shot trying to apprehend a gang of vicious ruffians some years ago.'

'Yes.' Tansy spoke blankly, surprised by the sudden cordiality in the other's tone.

'Inspector Clark was only a constable when I knew him,' Mrs Fletcher said, opening the door to its fullest width. 'Do please step in! Come into the drawing-room, Miss Clark.'

Somewhat bemused Tansy followed her into a large room so crowded with small tables and plants towering in tall pots that it seemed smaller than it actually was.

'Do please take a seat!' Mrs Fletcher took out a handkerchief and dusted a chair with some ceremony.

'Thank you.' Tansy sat down. 'I am here to make some enquiries about a gentleman who lodges with you.'

'Ah! Your esteemed father still takes an interest in crime! Keeps his mind active I daresay! I read about the shooting in the newspaper more than ten years ago and was most upset to learn of it. A true gentleman was your father!'

'May I ask where you knew him?' Tansy said puzzled. 'To my knowledge he has never mentioned—'

'It was a long time ago,' Mrs Fletcher said, seating herself on an adjoining chair. 'I was a young, innocent girl, an orphan and in great perplexity of mind as to what to do in life. I was in the large stores – one thinks more clearly while strolling among retail goods – and as I emerged a man grabbed my arm. A brute of a fellow, Miss Clark! You may imagine how terrified I was!'

'Yes indeed but—' Tansy tried to stem the flow.

'Then your father was there, very smart in his uniform! I cannot adequately express the relief of it, Miss Clark! But would you believe it? The dreadful individual who had accosted me actually accused me of stealing a length of lace! As I had passed the counter I must have have brushed against it and it had adhered to my pocket. Of course I tried to explain this and your father was most sympathetic. He quite understood how such an unfortunate mistake could have been made and paid for the lace out of his own pocket! I took a keen interest in his career after that. Indeed my luck soon changed and today I am a pillar of society.'

'Yes, I quite see that,' Tansy said gravely.

'So how can I help you?' Mrs Fletcher looked at her enquiringly.

'I understand you have a gentleman by the name of Curry staying here?'

'Yes indeed. Mr Michael Curry. He's a photographer.'

'I wondered how long he'd been away from his rooms,' Tansy said.

'Away? Mr Curry hasn't been away this summer,' Mrs Fletcher said. 'He sometimes goes to the east coast – the wildlife in the Essex marshes interests him but so far this year he—'

'But he hasn't been to his studio for several days,' Tansy broke in.

'Where else would he go?' Mrs Fletcher enquired. 'He has been out and about more than usual I will concede and why should he not, being as he's a single gentleman? However he always calls good-night as he goes up the stairs.'

'I have a photograph?' Tansy took it out of her bag.

'Let me adjust my spectacles!' Mrs Fletcher did so and took the photograph. 'Ah, now I see.'

'See what?' Tansy said.

'This is a photograph of Mr Wilks, who is Mr Curry's assistant.'

'It has this address on the back,' Tansy said blankly.

'Ladymead Gardens.' Mrs Fletcher turned the photograph over. 'No number you see. This house is divided into two. This is actually the back of the original very large dwelling-place. The front part is also a lodging house – number one, whereas we are number two. Mr Wilks lodges at number one. If you go down the side path and turn left you will see the house quite clearly. It has no garden which is why I preferred to buy this one.'

'Mr Wilks wears gold-rimmed spectacles,' Tansy said.

'Mr Curry wears gold-rimmed spectacles,' the other corrected as she handed back the photograph. 'His eyes are rather weak – from being so often in the darkroom, I suppose. That photograph is not of Mr Curry, Miss Clark, but of his assistant, Mr Wilks. I believe his first name is Thomas.'

'Has Mr Curry returned home yet this evening?' Tansy asked.

'No. He sometimes stays late at the studio, developing his photographs,' Mrs Fletcher said. 'I cannot understand how you could mistake Mr Curry for Mr Wilks!'

Because he identified himself as Mr Wilks, Tansy thought. Aloud she said: 'Mrs Fletcher, I would take it as a favour if you didn't mention my visit here. Obviously there's been some mistake and I will go and resolve it, but I'd not want anyone to think—'

'Not one word,' Mrs Fletcher said, rising. 'Not one syllable will pass my lips, Miss Clark. I have long owed your father a favour so it pleases me to oblige his daughter.'

'Thank you. I shall certainly convey my indebtedness to you to my father when I next see him,' Tansy responded. 'My apologies for troubling you. Good evening to you, ma'am.'

So Mr Curry had passed himself off as his assistant. The photograph he had given her was of that assistant. Tansy walked thoughtfully down the path and turned into the street. Where then was Mr Wilks?

Into her mind came the picture of a man tied to a water wheel. Had that been Mr Wilks, killed and tied up to deceive Verity and others that he was John Simpson? In that case who was the Philip Johnson who had sent notes to herself and to Henry Oakley? Who had flung the stones at her on two separate occasions?

She turned into Regent Street, now illumined by many street lamps and walked in the direction of the studio. Though it was past closing time Mr Curry, as she must now think of him, hadn't returned to his lodging.

The blinds had been pulled down over the window of the studio and when she tried the door it resisted her attempt to open it.

She turned away and walked on towards the nearest cab-stand. If Mr Curry was pretending to be Mr Wilks then he was obviously part of what was going on.

Arriving home and letting herself in without either Tilde or Mrs Timothy coming into the hall to greet her gave her a curiously abandoned feeling. She closed the door behind her, glad that she had left a couple of lamps burning. The house felt chilly as if summer was coming to an end.

Something brushed against her shoe. Tansy bent and picked

up the envelope on which her name was neatly printed.

Taking it into the sitting-room she sat down and carefully broke the seal with her nail. The message inside was brief.

Dear Miss Clark,

I cannot continue with this. I accepted a wager but I had no idea of the implications. I shall be in your back garden since I don't wish to be seen from the road. If you are not in when I come, that is. If you are in then I can explain why not only my conscience troubles me but I am indeed very much afraid.

Sincerely,

M. Curry.

Tansy pushed the letter and envelope into her drawer. For an instant she hesitated, then cautiously stepped to the french window and drew back the curtains. Light from the room flooded the terrace and the half-dozen steps leading down to the lawn.

'Mr Curry?'

Her voice died into the gloom beyond reach of the light just as a dark figure moved in a crouching run from one bush to the next.

But it might not be Mr Curry. Mr Curry might not have written the desperate little note at all! Or he might have written it in an effort to draw her out of the house into the garden which suddenly seemed too near to the river.

The ringing of the front doorbell filled her with relief. She swished the curtains back into place and went quickly to the front door. Perhaps Frank had completed his assignment and was ready to resume their friendship again.

She opened the door with a scolding quip on her lips only to see the immaculately clad Henry Oakley who doffed his hat as he said, 'Forgive me for disturbing you, Miss Clark, but may I come in?'

FOURTEEN

'Mr Oakley, please do so!' Tansy opened the door wider and stood aside.

'It's unpardonably late to call upon you, I know.' He stepped inside. 'I've made the necessary enquiries and I thought you would wish to learn the results as soon as possible.'

'Indeed I do!' Tansy closed the door and ushered her visitor into the sitting-room. 'I'm afraid you find me alone and servant-less. My housekeeper and my maid have taken themselves off to the music hall.'

'This is a charming room,' he said, glancing round with appreciation. 'It makes my own bachelor quarters seem sadly dull.'

'May I offer you something to drink? A whisky?' She was fast regaining her equilibrium.

'A small whisky-and-water would be very acceptable, but first let me set your mind at rest. Mr Curry is safe and sound and rather perturbed to discover that he had been missing at all.'

'Mr Curry,' Tansy said, 'was passing himself off as his own assistant, Mr Wilks! That can only mean the drowned man was Mr Wilks.'

'That's rather a far-fetched notion, Miss Clark!' He seated himself and shook his head.

'Then who else was it?' Tansy demanded.

'Some derelict who lost hope?'

'And drowned himself wearing John Simpson's clothes except for his shoes? Mr Oakley, it simply doesn't make sense!'

'Could John Simpson have faked his own death?' he suggested.

'Why?'

'He may have had debts we know nothing about, or perhaps his marriage was not as happy as we have been led to believe.'

'If he faked his own death how did he end up in the trunk?' Tansy demanded. 'If you fake your own death you go away somewhere, surely? And it would be an amazing coincidence if another man went and killed himself wearing clothes exactly similar to yours.'

'I agree. It doesn't sound logical,' he said.

'And please don't tell me that I didn't see John Simpson in the trunk, because I did!'

'I'm sure you did – and as you say—' He frowned.

'Chelsea cannot be swarming with unidentified corpses!' Tansy went on.

'Perhaps – no, that wouldn't do.'

'What wouldn't do? Oh, I'm sorry! I'll get you the water for your whisky! Pa complains that I always argue too readily.'

'You have a logical mind,' Oakley approved. 'I am sure you did see John Simpson's body in a trunk.'

'And when the police arrived there the trunk wasn't to be seen. It was moved to prevent its discovery!'

'But who on earth moved it?' he asked, puzzled. 'Mrs

Simpson isn't a tall, strong woman, is she?'

'Small and slender,' Tansy told him.

'And you're sure she didn't know you found it?'

'She had no idea I was even there!'

'You didn't drop your flowers on the way out?'

'I can't remember what I did with them,' Tansy confessed. 'All I could think about was getting home again as quickly as possible. Let me get you that water!'

She hurried into the kitchen and lit the lamp there, filled a jug with water, paused to give the aspidistra plant on the windowsill a quick splash. The plant was Mrs Timothy's pride and joy, though for her own part she agreed with Tilde that flowering plants added colour to a room.

Flowers? What was it about flowers that had suddenly tapped at the doors of her mind? Flowers.

'Here you are and my apologies for being so slow!' She poured out the whisky and took a tiny measure herself.

'It looks as if the mystery still remains then,' Oakley said.

'I know what I saw,' Tansy repeated obstinately. 'I don't suppose that I'll be called to give evidence at the inquest tomorrow but I do hate unfinished stories.'

She moved to the french windows and drew back the curtain a little, looking out into the darkness, but no figure moved there. Flowers? What was it she needed to remember about flowers?

'Miss Clark, is something wrong?' Oakley had risen and come to her side. 'You seem discomposed.'

'Before you came I thought I saw someone moving about in the garden,' Tansy said worriedly.

'Would you like me to take a look for you?'

'No, wait and I'll come with you,' she decided. 'I'll just get a cloak from my room. Please help yourself to another whisky. I have visitors so seldom that I forget how to be a proper hostess!'

She went up the stairs into her room and reached down her cloak from the wardrobe. Mr Oakley had sounded as if he were humouring a woman with an overheated imagination when he had offered to look round the garden for her. But there had been someone out there. There had! Impulsively she drew out the top drawer of the small locker by her bed. Wrapped in a large handkerchief the pistol her father had insisted upon giving her when she had resolved to move into the house Geoffrey had left her resided there untouched, save when once a month she took the trouble to clean it. In a small box at the side were half a dozen bullets.

'Remember to cock the pistol before you fire and don't ever fire until you have your target in your sights,' Laurence had advised.

'I don't intend ever to fire at anything that can move,' she had informed him.

'You might feel differently if you catch a burglar making off with your silver!' he had retorted. 'And if that should happen aim low for the legs! No sense in killing anyone!'

In the ten years she had lived here she had never needed the weapon, nor did she need it now since Henry Oakley was obviously eager to be of service to her. And she doubted very much if he walked around with a pistol in his pocket.

She had loaded the pistol as the thoughts passed through her mind, snapping on the safety catch and slipping it into the pocket of her dress under the light cloak.

Going downstairs and into the sitting-room she saw that Oakley had remained by the windows and was peering out.

'The moon's emerging,' he said, turning slightly as she came in. 'If there is a prowler he'll be the more easily seen. I wish you would stay within – some of these fellows can be nasty.'

Half of her would have been more than willing to stay indoors while he searched the long garden, patterned now with moonlight, but pride forbade it.

'I shall feel safer with you than in the house alone,' she said.

'As you please.'

He shot her a faintly amused look as they went out on to the terrace. The light from the sitting-room lamps and the moonlight made the scene almost as bright as day. Tansy could see the bushes outlined spikily against the pale background, hear in the quietness the murmuring of the river.

'You have a lovely garden,' he said softly.

'Yes. Yes, it's peaceful.' She kept her own voice low.

'And no sign of prowlers!'

'I daresay he's long gone,' she admitted.

'This must look charming in sunlight. Do you have anyone to help you with it?'

'I have someone come by to trim the hedges now and then but otherwise I rather enjoy grubbing about in the soil myself.'

She stumbled slightly, all her senses alert and aware.

You didn't drop your flowers on the way out? Henry Oakley had said that just before she went to get the water for his whisky.

But I never mentioned that I'd picked some flowers as an excuse to go back there, Tansy thought. I'm certain I didn't!

Henry Oakley? The suave publisher who had rejected John Simpson's manuscript? Henry Oakley who had arrived so opportunely just as someone flung a stone at her? Henry Oakley who had called upon her this evening to find out how much she was beginning to guess?

'I must have been mistaken!' she said breathlessly now. 'I can find no sign of anyone having been out here.'

'Better to be safe than sorry, Miss Clark! They may be hiding behind the wall.'

His hand was beneath her elbow and he was gently and inexorably urging her on down the garden towards the low wall beyond which the river murmured.

'One moment! I need a handkerchief!'

She slipped her free hand into her pocket and felt the comforting and solid weight of the pistol.

They had reached the low wall. All about her the bushes rustled in the full glory of their summer coverings.

'There isn't anyone here,' she said.

'Shall we walk along the bank and make absolutely certain?' he suggested.

'I really don't think—'

'And you can tell me exactly what it was that you recalled a few moments ago?'

Tansy stopped in her tracks, jerking her arm free. 'Flowers!' she said recklessly. 'You said that I might have dropped my flowers in Verity's kitchen when I left after finding the body. I never told you that I'd taken some flowers back as an excuse for returning. So how did you know about them?'

'I think you're getting a little muddled,' Oakley said in a soothing tone. 'I am quite certain you mentioned flowers.'

'No, I did not!'

She stepped warily away from him and felt something crunch under her feet.

Everything was moving in slow motion. She bent down and took up the shattered pieces of the gold-rimmed spectacles that lay in the grass, holding them out as their rims glinted in the moonlight.

'Mr Curry left a note for me before I came home this evening,' she said breathlessly. 'He told me that he would wait in my garden, that he was no criminal but had merely done what he did for a wager! What wager, Mr Oakley? Pretending to be his own assistant when I went into the shop? These are his spectacles, Mr Oakley! Was Mr Wilks the man tied to the wheel?'

'Miss Clark, you really aren't making much sense!' Oakley said, a slight impatience roughening his voice. 'What could I possibly have to do with a couple of photographers? Do try to be sensible!'

'Where is the man who wore these spectacles?' she demanded. 'No, don't come any closer! I have a pistol.'

She dragged it from her pocket, thrusting back the folds of her cloak.

'My dear Miss Clark!'

'My father,' she said, steadying her voice with an effort, 'taught me many things, Mr Oakley – how to pick out salient features in a person's appearance so they could be recognized long afterwards, how to weigh possibilities against probabilities, how to prime, load, cock and fire a pistol!'

She was still moving away from him, trying to reckon the distance that separated them, aware that the moonlight could alter size and shape, conscious also that she was more afraid of killing someone than of missing them.

'Miss Clark, you're not going to shoot me, you know.' His voice sounded silky soft.

'Mr Curry – the man who pretended to me to be Mr Wilks – where is he?' she demanded. 'What wager did he make?'

'A perfectly innocent wager.' He sounded amused again. 'We had other plans for Mr Wilks, plans of which he and Mr Curry were happily unaware. Mr Curry's photographic career is not doing as well as he hoped – you probably noticed that the photographs on the wall and in the window were not ones which were exactly recent, so when he was offered the opportunity to earn three hundred pounds simply for replacing his assistant over a few days he was happy to accept.'

'And the real Mr Wilks? He was killed, wasn't he?'

'My dear Miss Clark, if you think that I am going to stand here explaining the whys and wherefores while you wait in vain for help to arrive you are sadly mistaken!'

He finished with a subtle movement towards her which for an instant almost deceived her and then she was backing away, feeling the prickly leaves of a bush at her back, pulling the trigger with hands that shook uncontrollably, hearing above the murmuring of the river the loud cry of pain as the bullet hit its mark.

A moment's hesitation and he lunged towards her. Tansy fired wildly and long slivers of bark flew out of a nearby tree. Then she was over the low wall without any memory of having gone that way, running along the riverbank where the moonlight silvered the water and the whispering of the river sounded more like quarrelling as the night wind rose. Behind her she could hear Henry Oakley stumbling and limping as she fled.

She risked a look behind her and saw that despite his injury he was gaining on her. She could see the slow-moving wheel as it turned in the water and glimpsed also out of the corner of her eye another figure moving by the broken gate of The Larches.

Tansy fired again towards the crouching figure and heard the sharp crack of the bullet as it buried itself in the gatepost.

'That,' said Frank, rising from one knee, 'almost got me! Oakley, don't go on being a fool! There are police further along the bank!' Oakley had hesitated and then, with an oath, he went down the bank into the water, holding out his arms at each side of him as he tried to keep his balance in the swiftly flowing current.

There were lamps bobbing along the bank, helmeted figures running towards the wading figure.

'I think I'm going to faint or something,' Tansy said, gasping.

'Faint when you get indoors,' Frank advised, gingerly taking the pistol from her grasp. 'Come on, Tansy girl!'

FIFTEEN

'I'm fine now!' She spoke with trembling dignity, gently disengaging herself from his grasp. 'I have decided that I'm not the fainting type after all.'

'You're not the shooting type either,' Frank said. 'Never try to turn highwaywoman or you might shoot your own horse!'

'What I would like to know,' Tansy said, as they entered the house, 'is where you've been this last couple of days! Pa said you were off gathering information somewhere or other.'

'Sit yourself down and I'll get us both a brandy,' he said.

'Frank! Don't make me wait for explanations,' she begged, sinking into one of the chairs.

It was a peculiar feeling to be in her comfortable sitting-room where nothing had changed even though almost everything else seemed to have been stood on its head.

'Now!' She took a gulp of the brandy he handed her and she sat bolt upright, fixing him with a questioning eye.

'I've been looking into the background of the Simpson case,' Frank said, seating himself on another chair.

'How?'

'Your father suggested it. You know his rule about tracing events back to their beginning. So I took a railway trip to the Midlands and spoke to Verity Simpson's great-aunt.'

'But she's just died,' Tansy said blankly.

'Her Aunt Caroline is very much alive. The news of her death and of Verity's inheritance was somewhat premature – once little Mrs Simpson believed she had inherited property and a comfortable sum of money we reckoned she would betray herself.'

'Finn!' Tansy interrupted him as the manservant loped up the steps and came through the open french windows.

'Oakley in custody?' Frank enquired.

'Oakley very much in custody!' Finn said solemnly. 'He is also bloomin' wet from trying to swim across the river. Not a pretty sight!'

'Finn, what on earth are you doing here?' Tansy demanded.

'I've been lurking in the garden,' he returned. 'Keeping an eye on your wellbeing, so to speak.'

'I knew I'd seen somebody there!' Tansy exclaimed.

'I don't lurk as clever as I used to,' Finn apologized.

'Help yourself to a brandy.' Tansy nodded towards the decanter. 'Frank, please go on! What has Verity Simpson to do with all this?'

'Verity was brought up by her great-aunt,' Frank said. 'She was given a good education and acquired various accomplishments and her aunt hoped that she'd make a good marriage. Unfortunately she met Henry Oakley.'

'How? If she lived in the Midlands—'

'He went up to hunt for local writing talent, got invited to a few balls and dinner parties and met Verity.'

'And she was very much taken with 'im,' Finn said, relishing his brandy.

'Her Aunt Caroline was furious and greatly disapproved of her niece seeing him.'

'But why?' Tansy looked at them both. 'Henry Oakley is a respected publisher!'

'His father had been a respected publisher,' Frank corrected. 'Henry Oakley did try to continue the business but he has a taste for fine wines and fast racehorses. That was the main objection Verity's aunt had against him. So the romance came to an end and Oakley returned to London though I suspect that he and Verity kept up a correspondence.'

'Where does John Simpson come in?' Tansy enquired.

'Verity met him up in Birmingham but that romance was even less to her great aunt's liking. John Simpson was a young man who aspired to be a writer, having given up the notion of going to sea. A bit of a dreamer!'

'And Verity fell in love with him?'

'Verity is more in love with herself than with anyone else,' Frank said. 'She seems to have been attracted to him, however, but her aunt again objected so she persuaded him to elope with her. Her aunt was furious and sent word that Verity was disinherited until she was either separated or widowed.'

'That sounds very harsh,' Tansy said.

'Verity's aunt,' Frank said wryly, 'is a formidable lady. Verity meanwhile, on coming to London, met up with Henry Oakley again. I suspect they'd been constantly in touch all the time!'

'And her husband was writing a book,' Tansy said.

'She probably encouraged him to submit it to Oakley,' Frank

told her. 'It's my guess that John Simpson knew nothing of her previous relationship with him. Anyway, Verity hoped to persuade Oakley to accept the manuscript but Oakley came up with a better idea. John Simpson could fake his own death and lie low until Verity had been reinstated in her aunt's will.'

'The problem,' Finn said, 'was to find a corpse.'

'The morgue?' Tansy hazarded.

'I'm afraid stealing bodies from morgues is almost impossible. They do keep careful account. So someone had to be killed.'

'Mr Wilks from the photographic studio! It had to be!'

'Verity and her husband had had their wedding photograph taken in Curry's studio, so he was persuaded into what he believed was a wager – he would pass himself off as his own assistant in the studio while Mr Wilks was "on holiday" as they put it.'

'Surely Mr Curry suspected some mischief was afoot?' Tansy said.

'He were a bit short of the readies,' Finn contributed.

'So Mr Curry's studio wasn't prospering and he didn't ask too many questions about the wager?' Tansy shook her head. 'What about his assistant?'

'He was invited round to The Larches,' Frank said. 'We don't know exactly what excuse was used to take him there – the prospect of a lucrative commission perhaps? Mr Curry meanwhile went round to Wilks's lodgings and told the landlady his assistant had gone away for a long holiday. Then he simply pretended to be him when he went to the studio. Wilks was a shy young man with no close family and no real friends. He wouldn't be readily missed and, more important, he was the same height and colouring as John Simpson.'

'And John Simpson and Verity killed him? John Simpson was

a murderer, then? And I've been feeling sorry for him!' Tansy said indignantly.

'John Simpson was bewitched almost equally between Verity and the prospect of her inheritance,' Frank said.

'So John Simpson struck him hard enough to render him unconscious and then the hapless Mr Wilks was dressed in Simpson's clothes and the engraved wedding ring forced on his finger.'

'But the shoes were too small!' Tansy said.

'So the shoes were left off and since his own shoes had a rather distinctive pattern on the soles they were tossed into the river. A lad fishing some way downstream found them only this morning and had the good sense to hand them over to a policeman because he thought it was odd for someone to throw a perfectly good pair of shoes away.'

'And then they – Verity and her husband – took Mr Wilks out to the water wheel and tied him there to finish him off and to suggest that he'd committed suicide?'

'I think it's more likely that Oakley carried out the final details,' Frank said thoughtfully. 'Simpson was a poor swimmer and I can't see Verity swimming out with an unconscious body in tow!'

'Far too ladylike and delicate,' Tansy murmured.

'But nasty with it,' Finn said cheerfully.

'So Wilks drowned,' Frank continued. 'The poor fellow must've struggled frantically – perhaps the shock of the cold water caused him to begin to regain consciousness but Oakley must've held him under and once he was certain he was dead tied him to the water wheel. The spokes would have done the rest.'

'That was done – when?' Tansy sat up straighter. 'There was nothing on that water wheel when I first saw Verity.'

'That's true!' Finn grimaced. 'Look! he was definitely drowned. The autopsy proved that. Maybe they simply held his head down in a bath of water and took him to the water wheel a couple of hours before the fisherman arrived on the bank and started fishing.'

'And Simpson was in town on the night that Mr Wilks was killed. That was where I saw him from the cab window!'

'You were right about that.' Frank nodded at her. 'Maybe he couldn't face being around for the actual murder?'

'He still knew it was being carried out. He must have known. But he went along with what his wife and Oakley planned. I wouldn't waste too much sympathy on him if I were you!'

'I am not wasting any sympathy on any of them,' Tansy said.

'So Oakley killed Mr Wilks while John Simpson – stayed in town?'

'Took a room at the White Bull under another name for a couple of nights – they're not too fussy about checking out identities there,' replied Frank.

'But someone sent me a letter asking me to meet him there – a Philip Johnson – and Henry Oakley got a similar letter!'

'Tansy girl, think back.' Frank said.

'A little lad shoved the note into my hand. It was a chance to prove that I hadn't been imagining things when I had glimpsed John Simpson,' Tansy said slowly. 'So I went at once.'

'Not telling a soul!' Finn said disapprovingly. 'Your Pa and I would not have been pleased!'

'I went anyway,' Tansy said. 'I saw someone – a figure in the yard at the side of the White Bull and – I think something about it did remind me of John Simpson, so I followed and then he flung a stone—'

'And Oakley was suddenly there! Tansy, are you sure you know who threw the stone?'

'It was very dark and there were footsteps and then – I'm not sure now where it came from,' she admitted. 'I was just so relieved to see Henry Oakley!'

'It's my guess that it was Oakley who threw the stone – same as the stone that was thrown over the hedge in the park? Meant to give you a fright more than anything I reckon,' Frank said. 'Warn you off any more delving. Remember Oakley had seen you with me when I was asking about John Simpson's manuscript. And he knew you were the daughter of a respected police officer. He tried to warn you off and then he sent you that mysterious letter under the name of Philip Johnson, hoping to lure you out to the White Bull.'

'Where John Simpson was staying.'

'So either the stone would hit you in which case you might have been fished up out of the Thames in a few days' time or it wouldn't hit you and he could rush forward as your saviour, with a note ostensibly to him in his pocket. Where is your note from the mysterious Philip Johnson who never existed in the first place?'

'Henry Oakley said that he'd take both notes to the police.' she said wryly.

'Needless to say the police received nothing. But the whole episode made you trust Oakley more, didn't it?'

'It never occurred to me not to trust him,' Tansy said. 'He was the publisher who had rejected the manuscript as far as I was concerned.'

'But for all he knew you were hot on his trail! So he had to set up a little pantomime in order to find out how much you knew.'

'And I walked straight into the trap he set,' Tansy said ruefully.

'I've played billiards with him on more than one occasion,' Frank said with a grin.

'How did you know about the notes?' Tansy demanded suddenly. 'I never said anything because I knew you'd disapprove of my going off by myself to find out things.'

'Verity told us,' Frank said.

'Verity! Then she—'

'Was taken in for questioning earlier this evening. She panicked and laid all the blame on Oakley.'

'Why didn't you come and tell me?' Tansy said indignantly. 'You told me the police found nothing – no trunk, no body, nothing!'

'The trunk was found later. You cannot guess where?'

Tansy shook her head.

'At the bottom of your garden,' Frank said, looking amused. 'Oakley was in the house with her when you called.'

'I knew there was somebody!'

'And you left some flowers in the kitchen, so they guessed you'd gone back and let yourself in the back way. They simply carried the trunk along the riverbank and put it at the bottom of your garden while the police and Finn searched The Larches. When the police left they carried it back and it went off as luggage in the carriage they'd previously hired.'

'So why wasn't Henry Oakley arrested at once?'

'There was only Verity Simpson's word that he was involved at all. The police wanted further proof. They kept a discreet eye on him.'

'Mr Curry – the real Mr Curry who took a wager and pretended to be his assistant, Mr Wilks – I found his spectacles in the garden.' Tansy shivered slightly.

'You were out so he slipped a note through your door and went round to the back in case Oakley had followed him there. Oakley turned up, followed him, there was a struggle—'

'Then Mr Curry is dead too?'

'He 'as a nasty bang on 'is bonce, Miss Tansy,' Finn put in. 'Oakley left 'im for dead just afore we rolled up.'

'You came the back way along the bank? I was letting myself in at the front,' Tansy said. 'Henry Oakley must have hurried round to my front door and rung the bell while I was wondering who was lurking in the back!'

'I said as 'ow I'm out of practice with the lurking,' Finn said apologetically. 'I'm out of practice on account of becoming so law-abiding!'

'So, having been forbidden to marry Henry Oakley she eloped with John Simpson, persuaded him to fake his own death by having someone else killed and was so clever that John Simpson never suspected that once he was officially dead there was no bar to her having him killed too?'

'Little Mrs Simpson has a tremendous amount of charm,' Frank said. 'It's my belief that having persuaded both John Simpson and Henry Oakley to go along with her scheme she might, with Simpson out of the way, have found means to rid herself of Oakley too before long.'

'I thought she'd had a romance with him!'

'The only real romance Verity Simpson has is with herself and with the promised legacy from her aunt.'

'Poor aunt!' Tansy exclaimed.

'She's a tough old lady,' Frank said.

'I'd best be off. Your pa will want to know 'ow it all turned out,' Finn said. 'Excuse me asking, Miss Tansy, but 'ow comes it that you're 'ere all alone?'

'Mrs Timothy and Tilde went out to the music hall together,' Tansy said.

'So I'm not to 'ave the pleasure of meeting the estimable lady? Another time perhaps!'

With which hope Finn took his long body and longer face through the french windows again.

'I wonder why Henry Oakley came here tonight,' Tansy said, getting up to lock the windows.

'I suspect he wasn't very happy about your having been absolutely convinced by his story and he must have wondered when he saw Mr Curry sneaking round the back. Maybe he even saw him slip in the note so he went round the back, attacked him and finished him off, as he hoped, and then saw the lamps go on in the house and came round to the front to knock on the door as if he'd just arrived. By then we'd found Curry and Finn was in the back garden.'

'And you all knew that I was here with a vicious killer!'

'I'd back you against a vicious killer any time,' Frank said affectionately. 'Tell me, do you usually wander round with a pistol in your pocket? If so I shall worry about you less in future!'

'Do you worry about me, Frank?'

Her voice had softened as she turned to him.

'Sometimes – most of the time. Why the pistol?'

'Oakley let slip that he knew I'd dropped some flowers in the kitchen where the trunk was hidden, so he knew that I'd been there.'

'And he guessed that you'd picked up the mistake he'd made?'

'Which is why he suggested a walk in the garden.'

'And you took the pistol with you. '

'Was there really a manuscript?' Tansy came and sat down again.

'There was indeed! It was under the mattress in the room he'd taken at the White Bull. A romance which apparently isn't too badly written. '

'He really hoped to get it published then?'

'But Verity advised him to submit it to Henry Oakley. The pair of them had obviously kept in touch after her great-aunt forbade their relationship. What Oakley and Verity wanted was to get John Simpson out of the way so she wouldn't lose her eventual inheritance.'

'Then why not simply kill him instead of setting up such an elaborate scheme?' Tansy queried.

'Because it had to look like suicide and that's hard to fake. Simpson agreed to fake his own death and if he wasn't directly involved in the murder of Mr Wilks he certainly knew that a body would have to be obtained somehow or other, so I wouldn't waste too much sympathy on him if I were you!'

'And Mr Curry unwittingly helped them by accepting a wager that he couldn't pass himself off as his own assistant! Of course he was aided by the fact that his photographic business wasn't doing well and he certainly had no regular customers.'

'And he didn't link the wager with the so-called suicide at first because he told me about John Simpson being left-handed.'

'It was almost certainly afterwards that he began to worry about what lay behind the wager.'

'And came here. How did he know my address?'

'Lord knows! Maybe he followed you? We'll find out when his

head stops aching!' Frank said.

'What about the inquest tomorrow?' Tansy asked. 'I suppose I might be called to give evidence?'

'Certainly you will. Why?'

'What on earth does one wear to an inquest?' Tansy worried. 'Black? That would be suitable I suppose but black really isn't my best colour. Green? A nice dark green?'

She broke off as Frank started to laugh.

'Is something amusing you?' She gave him a stony look.

'You!' Frank said. 'You rush into strange places without even telling your closest friends where you're going! You happily pack a pistol though you've never fired at anybody in your life and take a moonlight stroll with a man you're just realizing is a vicious killer! You, my darling Tansy, amuse me more every time we meet!'

The sound of the front door opening interrupted her retort.

'I'm that sorry we're so late!' Mrs Timothy cried, sweeping into the room with Tilde at her heels. 'It was a marvellous show! Really very tasteful and afterwards we indulged ourselves with a pie-and-mash supper and a small glass of sweet sherry – not that I generally indulge, but it being a special occasion and – Tilde, go and put the kettle on! Good evening, Mr Frank! Will you be wanting a cup of tea?'

'It's time I was going,' Frank said. 'Shall I call for you tomorrow – for the inquest?'

'Yes – thank you,' Tansy said slightly bemused.

'Come along, Tilde! Time we got back down to earth,' Mrs Timothy said briskly.

'It was lovely!' Tilde breathed as she obeyed. 'The ladies in the show wore spangled dresses with feather plumes in their hair!

Ever so elegant they were!'

'Your problem's solved,' Frank told Tansy. 'Spangles and feathers would suit you admirably!'

'I shall wear green,' Tansy told him. 'Go home, Frank!'

'Until tomorrow then!'

He was at the door when she said:

'That word you used before – did you mean it?'

'What word?'

'Darling.' To her annoyance she found herself blushing.

'You guess!' He blew a kiss and sauntered out, leaving her blushing in her pretty room.